The Dogman Epoch II:
The Edge of Night

To Logan —
Beyond the Edge of Night!

Jh Hd

The Dogman Epoch II: The Edge of Night

Frank Holes, Jr.

ISBN: 1533351155
ISBN-13: 978-1533351159

To order copies, please visit our website:
http://www.mythmichigan.com

To all my family –
Thanks for all the unwavering support.
I love you all.

Also by Frank Holes, Jr.

Year of the Dogman
The Haunting of Sigma
Nagual: Dawn of the Dogmen
Tales From Dogman Country

The Dogman Epoch: Shadow and Flame

The Longquist Adventures: Western Odyssey
The Longquist Adventures: Viking Treasure

Find all of Frank's books on our website:

http://www.mythmichigan.com

PROLOGUE

Heavy fog and mist concealed most of the land, though the largest of the drooping tree branches could be seen here and there, like the hairy arms of gigantic spiders whose bodies were still hidden well behind thick, intricate webs. A dense layer of dark, low-hanging clouds lay like an enveloping blanket just over the fog, completely blocking out the sky above.

There would be no sunshine this day.

The early morning silence was broken by the long, wailing cry of a bird far off in the foliage.

On a game trail at the base of a tall and towering steep hill, a fat porcupine waddled its way toward the cover of the dense forest only a spear's throw away. The animal was in a hurry, not only because the dawn brought the light that provided its predators an advantage, but also because the land didn't smell quite right this morning. The smell of man was in the air, on the grass, on the faint tracks of the game trail. The porcupine knew that man was to be feared. Man would kill him and eat him even more quickly than the wolves, bears, and great cats, and there was no defending himself from man and his sharp spears that could easily reach beyond the length of the animal's quills.

Yes, the smell of man was all around, though the porcupine couldn't see him. The land was still, silent. Somewhere, man was hidden away, perhaps ready to pounce at any moment.

The porcupine heard a small cracking sound, away and up the steep hillside to its right, just the tiniest sound, like the breaking of a robin's egg that had fallen from the nest.

Alarmed, the animal froze, partially hidden behind a thick clump of grass. It stared up at the hillside, watching as a section of the earth moved. Part of the animal's simple brain screamed *Danger! Run!* But another part was ever so curious about the world. Being fairly well armed, the porcupine is generally allowed a bit more curiosity than other animals. So whereas other animals would have bolted immediately at seeing the hillside come to life, the porcupine was more than willing to watch for a few seconds.

That round spot of the hill, for it was nearly perfectly round, spun slowly counter-clockwise and then popped outward about a foot from the upward slope of the ground. Dirt shook and drifted downward, and a few small clumps and pebbles rolled a little way down the hill before coming to rest. The hillside wasn't steep enough to cause an avalanche, but it was certainly steep enough to discourage most animals from climbing it, either up or down.

The porcupine had never seen anything like this in its short life, and so it continued to stare. Something was climbing out from a hole in the hillside, hidden from sight by that dirty covering that resembled a flat, round leaf.

First, a pair of dirty brown legs cautiously reached out of the hole and found purchase on the sloping ground. Then a dirty brown hand and arm used the side of the hole for leverage. The creature emerged.

Immediately, the porcupine's sense of fear won out, and it scuttled down the trail as fast as its stumpy little legs could carry it. *Danger, danger, danger,* its little brain shouted over and over. *Run...man.*

Normally, a porcupine could move across the land without a sound, but this morning, as it hurried toward the safety of the forest, the instinct for flight took hold and the little animal made an awful racket—for a porcupine, that is—as it disappeared into the underbrush.

And not just one man did the porcupine see or hear. In dozens of places along the hillside, a cacophony of cracks preceded the emergence of an entire army of humans who had been in hiding, dug into concealed foxholes in the soft earth of the hill.

***

The night before, each warrior had carved out his foxhole in the hillside, just big enough for his body to fit snugly within. Then the warriors had painted over their shields with dirt, mud, grasses, and leaves to blend in with the hillside. Very carefully, they each used an evergreen branch to smooth over and erase their tracks in the dirt and grass. At their commander's signal, they had all retreated into the foxholes for the night, camouflaged perfectly and completely once their shields were in place.

Now, they were all wide-awake and ready for whatever the day would bring. Each man's eyes scanned the surroundings, and their senses were on high alert. They had been on the march for three days now, anticipating contact with their enemy at any point. Their battle would come soon; they could all feel it.

The Nagual were near, leading an army of evil men. They had been harrying the Good People of the high country for weeks. Tribes all around the foothills of the northern mountains were fleeing for their lives, as the Nagual kept no prisoners. None were left alive, and none joined their ranks. This evil army had but one purpose—the total annihilation of all humans in its path.

Village after village was destroyed—burned to the ground, the acrid smoke rising high into the still high country air. The few who had been fortunate to escape ran for their lives, scattered and leaderless.

And yet there was still a flicker of hope in the north. The Guardians of the great Elk Clan, the protectors of the white wisdom, assembled the warriors from every tribe that remained. Over 400 had answered the call. They were a mix of seasoned veterans and passionate youth who drilled and trained daily, hardened by the elements.

Within days of assembly, they had already hunted down and defeated several rogue bands of traitorous men, those with evil hearts who had joined the Nagual. They had even fought a handful of these Dogmen, though the creatures retreated when injured and greatly outnumbered.

Their eyes always burned with golden hatred, and their faces bore an intelligent, grimacing snarl before they turned tail and fled.

Yet every man in the Elk Clan army knew that there was a larger force, a true Nagual-led army rampaging through the land. It was a force comprised of dozens of Dogmen and hundreds (if not bordering on thousands) of evil human warriors.

And there were rumors of something else, something far more terrifying that accompanied the Nagual army—a gigantic beast, black as the moonless night, with eyes that danced with fire and a mouth full of needle-like teeth.

***

The warriors of the brown Elk Clan army said not a word, but cautiously tiptoed down the steep hill to the game trail below. Despite the dirt that clung to their bodies and hair, the men were hardened warriors who had become quickly used to living in such conditions without a second thought.

Each man looked identical, especially since they were dirty and dusty, and their individuality seemed to melt away. Thin thongs tied from their foreheads to the back of their necks kept their long hair out of their faces. Each man wore a simple leather sandal that laced up over the toes and heel and tied at the ankle. They preferred to go barefoot whenever possible, just like any other tribesman in the land, but training for and fighting in battles meant protecting the feet. The Elk Clan warriors also wore a simple skirting around the waist and hips. These were stitched around the legs and studded with beads and bones, the best armor one could hope for in that region of the body.

They all carried a round shield in one hand and a thick spear in the other. Covering their chests was a simple but effective armor fashioned of hardened strips of leather, wood, and bone, woven tightly with animal sinew.

Tied across each of their backs was a long pouch, almost like a quiver, which carried a dozen short throwing spears. Each of these spears was the length of a man's forearm, heavy for their size, and sharpened to precise, needle-like points.

Most of the warriors had been trained since youth to snatch a spear from behind the head and to sling it with deadly accuracy. These short spears also made formidable hand-to-hand weapons if the enemy got too close.

Spaced through the army were a dozen captains. These older warriors stood nearly a head taller than the rest, and they lacked the armor worn by the troops, only sharing the same simple skirt and sandals. But what truly set the captains apart were their braids. Their hair had been pulled back into a pair of long, tightly woven tails that were interspersed with small beads and feathers.

And around each captain's neck was a thin string, upon which a small tip of an elk's antler hung.

There was no milling about when they all assembled at the game trail at the base of the tall hill. There were no morning pleasantries or shared breakfasts. No smiles or laughs. There were no shouted orders from the captains. Instead, everyone silently partnered up, shield in one hand and long spear in the other.

The men marched in two lines, side-by side, with hardly a sound, following the game trail as it wound through the still forest. Their journey this morning would take them to a village at the southernmost point of the foothills. Little hope remained in the men's hearts that they would find any survivors there.

***

The sun would have climbed two arm lengths in the sky, had they been able to see it through the thick cloud cover, when a loud crack in the underbrush suddenly caught the attention of the entire army. In a moment, the warriors spun toward the noise and readied their shields and spears.

Not a sound was heard in the forest. No birds, no wind in the leaves, nothing. All eyes were fixed on the spot from which the sound had originated.

Without warning, the foliage to their left erupted, and a wave of assailants burst forth. Branches, ferns, and bracken shot in all directions as the enemy rushed forward.

Most were short, squatty men with hideous, screaming faces covered in smears of war paint. They carried short spears, knives, and crudely carved hatchets. They wore no armor, only a thick fur wrapping that covered their chests and waists.

Though the enemy outnumbered the Elk Clan army, the attackers were easily overmatched. Highly trained and disciplined, the Elk army stabbed and thrust their spears forward over and around the shields of their comrades in the front rank. The first wave of evil men lay in the underbrush, their cries of pain silenced quickly by well-placed thrusts of Elk warrior spears.

No Elk Clan casualties had resulted so far. The battle would have been over quickly if that was all that the enemy had to throw at them.

It was not.

***

A piercing pair of howls from deep in the treeline sent chills through the Elk Clan army. On the heels of the first wave, another battalion of enemy warriors charged, this time from both sides of the trail. The rear line of the Elk army swung around to meet this challenge, and now there was no backup.

Facing the enemy's new tactic, the captains of the Elk army all began to spasm, their bodies convulsing as they changed form. They grew to twice their normal size, thick fur sprouting over their otherwise smooth skin. Each captain's long braids stood upright and hardened into sharply pointed antlers. Additional tines protruded where each bead or feather had been previously woven into the hair. Their arms became muscular forelegs, their fists became hooves that pawed at the air before thundering down upon all fours.

These Elk Guardians, easily standing six feet at the shoulder, were ready to battle. And beyond their legendary strength and agility, each possessed a rack of antlers nearly a dozen feet across.

In the center of the line, their chieftain, the leader of the Elk Guardians, had already transformed into a massive creature that seemed more like a mighty moose than an elk like the captains. His body was an arm-spread in width, and a man could stand upright beneath his belly. His curved, leaf-shaped antler rack could plow a dozen men from his path with ease.

Bugling across the battle line to each other, the Guardians stamped and pawed the dirt, waiting as the next wave of the enemy approached.

***

Hundreds of the enemy sprinted into the fray, and soon the forest path was awash with the red blood of battle. Most were dispatched swiftly with the sharp point of a long spear. And the Guardians easily thrashed the dark men, impaling them or sending them crashing back into their brethren.

Before long, the attackers were forced to climb over the bodies of their fallen comrades. Others began to hurl rocks and logs from a safer distance.

Though well trained, the Elk Clan army was tiring. There was simply no end to the attackers. Wave after wave poured forth from the cover of the forest.

And then, as quickly as the battle had begun, there were no more attacks. The enemy soldiers who had yet to cross the barrier of bodies turned and fled back toward the trees.

The warriors of the Elk Clan, breathing heavily from the battle, looked to their Guardians. The 12 great elk stamped the ground, loud snorts issuing from their nostrils.

The Guardian chieftain in his majestic moose form trumpeted a bellow that echoed through the forest. At that signal, the entire Elk Clan army followed with their own war cries and pursued their enemy into the treeline.

It wasn't much effort to overcome the fleeing enemy. And for these warriors who had grown up living in and among the forest, there was no place for the enemy to hide where they wouldn't be found.

Soon the Elk Clan army was spread out throughout the forest, finishing off the last of their pursuits. The Guardians gave out loud trumpeting calls to regroup, but it was too late.

The trap had been sprung.

***

The Nagual appeared as if they had been hidden by some magical force. They leapt out of the tall ferns, snatching up Elk Clan warriors who had separated themselves from the main group. None had time to even scream out a warning. They just suddenly disappeared beneath the underbrush.

The Elk Guardians swung their huge heads side to side, sensing the change in the enemy's tactics. They trumpeted again and again to signal the army to fall back as more of their troops were taken down.

Their great Guardian chieftain also sensed something, a new presence, an evil presence, marching toward them from behind. It was the monster that the rumors had spoken of. The black beast of legend—what the ancient people had called the *Concua Cahuayoh*, the monster that devours everything in its path.

Turning his own massive body around to the rear, the gigantic Moose chieftain rallied his troops and the nearby Guardians to face this new devilry.

But well before the beast was even revealed, the Nagual made a full-out attack. The Dogmen's roars echoed through the trees. Their fangs and claws slashed and tore through leather, flesh, and bone. The human soldiers simply weren't fast enough on their own to take on a Dogman one on one.

In small pockets, those warriors fighting alongside an Elk Guardian fared better. More than one Nagual, as it had leapt high into the air, had been impaled upon a Guardian's sharp tines. Even the humans had managed to defeat several Dogmen, working together to stab them over and over with their sharp spears.

But it was not enough. The Elk army was already on its last legs. As quickly as one soldier paused to catch his breath, he was snatched away. Even the great Guardians were taken down, many falling beneath the ripping claws of a pack of Dogmen.

Soon there was only one pocket of resistance left—consisting only of a couple of dozen exhausted humans, four limping Elk Guardians, and their Moose chieftain.

Sensing their time had come, the Nagual charged. Racing on all four legs through the underbrush, they attacked this last group from all sides. This battle was short but intense, and in the end only the great chieftain remained, facing off with two Dogmen. And beyond these battling legends, the black beast remained, waiting its turn in the dark shadow of the forest.

The Dogmen circled the mighty Moose, snarling savagely. One feinted while the other leapt forward. Though the Guardian was quickly tiring, it easily deflected them both with a well-timed swing of its antlers and a swift kick of its rear legs.

Snorting loudly through his nostrils, the chieftain attempted to retreat. The two Nagual charged again, and he dispelled one with a quick jerk of his thick neck. The first enemy was knocked away in midair with the powerful antlers, its wolfish snout smashed back into its skull, bloody teeth flying in all directions. But the second Dogman was too quick for the exhausted Guardian. Though his head and rack whipped around, the Guardian's shoulder became the target for the Nagual, the claws of its hands and feet sinking deeply into the shaggy fur.

Since his antlers couldn't quite reach the attacker, the great chieftain shifted his weight and sidestepped, slamming his body against a great oak tree. The Nagual howled in pain as the bones of its lower body were completely crushed.

But the damage had been done. The Guardian chieftain staggered away from the Dogman and turned around, only to face the greatest enemy of their age.

Like something from a nightmare, the monstrous black beast stamped through the forest. Trees fell with but a shake from its powerful shoulders, hips, and tail. All around the creature, the world seemed to draw into darkness as if it were absorbing the light and life of its surroundings. It brought with it a profound coldness as well. In mere moments, the Moose Guardian could see his breath snorting out in cool clouds.

The beast dug the claws of its four feet into the soft soil of the forest floor. Its wide, half-moon mouth opened in a snarling smile, revealing rows of needle-like teeth. Its eyes glowed a fierce, demonic red.

And without warning, the *Concua Cahuayoh*, the beast of the darkness, lunged across the glade in the blink of an eye. The four muscular legs curled back with the agility of powerful arms, each ending with wide spread claws. For an instant, the air surging through the tall, stiff hairs of its back whistled, and then it was upon its prey.

The impact of the immense body of the *Concua* completely bowled over the Moose Guardian, and the two creatures rolled back through the underbrush. The Guardian used his weapons well, driving kick after kick of his rock-like hooves into the evil beast's belly and sides. Quick snaps of the head drove the tines of his antlers, thick as the spears of the warriors, deeply into his enemy's flesh.

But the *Concua Cahuayoh* proved too powerful. Even had the Guardian chieftain been at his full strength, it may have proved no match. The black beast snapped its jaws again and again, eventually clamping shut on the Guardian's left antler. In a sickening crunch, the bones were crushed and then ripped from the Moose's skull. The great Moose bellowed out one last time before the *Concua* tore into its throat. And then, only spastic wheezing could be heard from the mouth of one of the world's last great Guardians.

Gasping, loud and grating, was the only sound that could be heard in the still forest air.

Book 3
Disclosure

The Dogman Epoch II: The Edge of Night

Chapter 1

The gasping continued, loud and grating in Kaiyoo's ears. Only after a few seconds did the boy realize the noise was coming from his own mouth. As he finally noticed his friend Wayotel looking back at him in alarm, he took control of his jaw muscles and stopped, embarrassed.

It was all a dream.

Kaiyoo lay back down on the bed of soft pine needles and stared up at the dark gray cloudy sky above them. It was the same sky as in his dream. He covered his dirty young face with his two hands.

And yet, it was more than just a dream. Of that Kaiyoo was certain.

He had seen a vision, a glimpse into a horrible event that had happened this very morning somewhere in the wide land about them.

The Nagual were real. They were really here, running loose in the world, leaving a trail of destruction behind them.

And according to the dream, there was something else—dare he think it—even more awful that had been set free in their world. Something of monstrous size and unlimited power. Something with rows of needle-like teeth.

It meant that all the tales of his youth, passed down by Wa-Kama and even Tommakee the wanderer, were true. They weren't just horror stories told around the campfire to scare the young into staying inside at night. The evil creatures were real.

Of course that meant that everything from his last memory wasn't a dream either. Horrible event indeed! The vision he had seen was nothing compared to the unthinkable horror that had passed at the Guardian Council.

The great bears, the Guardians and protectors of the world, had been decimated, wiped out in one brief night's passing. The great city of Atolaco and all of the good people who had gathered there for the Sun Festival were undoubtedly annihilated in the massive fire.

It was too much to think about at that moment, and so Kaiyoo silently began to cry, his face hidden behind his dirty hands.

***

Wayotel stared at his friend for a few moments longer before finally exhaling. He had been so worried about the other boy that he had hardly thought about his own well-being. In his 11 years, he couldn't remember not having eaten for longer than a day. Indeed, now that he was sure his friend was okay, his stomach growled loudly. It had been quite a while since his last meal.

Both boys were filthy, their normally browned skin completely covered in dried gray mud and ash from head to toe. Little black cinders speckled both of their bodies.

Wayotel reflected on the amazing fact that they were alive at all. They had survived a raging forest fire, a surging river, and a plunge off of a waterfall that was twice the height of the world's tallest pine.

They had also avoided death at the claws of the Dogmen, who were right at their heels when the two boys leapt into the depths of the river.

They had witnessed the destruction of the world's greatest Guardians, the Nihuatl, the giant shape-shifting bears. As far as either boy knew, every single one of them was dead.

There was no one to stand up against the Nagual now. There was no one to protect the world.

But not all of the spirits of the world had been against them. They had managed to snag hold of the huge floating body of a dead Nihuatl, though they knew not which of the great bears it was. It was only in this way that they had been able to outdistance the conflagration around them. They held tightly to the Nihuatl's long fur as they went over the huge waterfall, keeping themselves from smashing on the rocks below and drowning.

And the greatest blessing was the rain that fell sometime in the night. The storm had moved through slowly, eventually drowning out the fire that would have otherwise been raging throughout the entire forest. It would have overswept the two boys, who having already survived so much, had collapsed in exhaustion on the riverbank.

Kaiyoo curled up on the ground, his face in his hands. His sobs were soon replaced by the deep breathing of sleep.

Wayotel also lay back down on the cool ground, suddenly aware too of how tired he was.

Somewhere overhead, a pair of birds chirped to each other.

***

The boys rested, Kaiyoo from weariness and Wayotel out of relief that his friend was indeed alive.

When they awoke, the sun was only just above the treetops, sending little shafts of muted light down to the boys below. Despite the warmth of the summer day, the evening air was already growing cool, each day now advancing them toward the long winter ahead.

Kaiyoo shivered. "Wish we could have a fire," he said aloud. "Probably shouldn't though. Those Nagual are still out there, somewhere. I can almost feel them."

The only response Wayotel gave was a little nod. He was sitting close by, but he didn't say anything. He didn't even look at Kaiyoo.

"You've been awake longer than me, haven't you." Kaiyoo stated more than asked. "How did we end up here?"

Wayotel absently drew lines in the soft earth with a stick. When he finally spoke, his voice was distant.

"You changed," he began, without looking up from the dirt. His voice was not much more than a whisper, and he spoke in short choppy sentences. "Sometime after we started falling. I'm not sure when it happened. I was screaming. My eyes were shut. We hit the water below. It tore the fur out of my hands. It took my breath from my chest.

"It was all dark, a blur. I opened my eyes. I was underwater. But it was too dark to see. I had no idea what way was up. And I can't swim, you know that." Wayotel's eyes were now watering. "I gulped in water. I was choking, drowning. My head was spinning. I thought for sure I was going to die."

Kaiyoo stared intently at his friend. "What happened? I don't remember anything."

"You saved me."

"Me? How?"

Looking up, Wayotel locked eyes with his friend. "I felt like I was falling, further and further from the surface. It was all over. Then there was a sharp, awful pain in my shoulder."

His right hand reached across his skinny brown chest and rubbed his left shoulder tenderly. "You had a hold of me. You were pulling me back up."

"I don't remember," said Kaiyoo.

"You weren't yourself. You'd changed. I don't think you could have pulled me back up if you'd been yourself."

"I was a..."

"A Nihuatl, yes." Wayotel gave a little chuckle, the first real sign of liveliness Kaiyoo had yet seen this day. "You've got quite a grip."

Confused, Kaiyoo tilted his head.

Wayotel pulled back the shredded remains of the shirt he'd been wearing. There were jagged, white streaks all across his shoulder—scars that would last the rest of his life.

"You'd locked on with your teeth and pulled me back to the surface."

"I'm sorry," Kaiyoo said, reaching out and tracing the scars with his fingers. "It must have hurt."

"Oh, it did," Wayotel said with a little pride. He had survived, after all. "You tugged me to shore, after fighting the current for what seemed forever. I could barely breathe, but with my shoulder in your big mouth, my head was up out of the water.

"You dragged us up right over there," Wayotel pointed to a spot a little down the hill from where they were sitting.

Kaiyoo could see clawed-up earth near the river's edge.

"I don't quite remember all of it," Wayotel continued. "I must have passed out sometime in the river. I remember my legs being dragged through mud and rocks. It was raining. I was lying right next to you—your fur was warm. But I can't remember seeing anything."

The skinny boy stared off at the bank of the Atolaco River below them for quite some time, lost in his own thoughts. Then he took a deep breath and continued.

"When I finally awoke, you'd changed back into yourself. That was when I knew you had saved me in the river. You had changed to save us both.

"I tried to wake you, but you just kept sleeping. I even dragged you up here away from the river. I was worried one of those Nagual might find us somehow. I pulled you up out of sight and covered us as best as I could."

Kaiyoo turned his head from where they were sitting down to the riverbank. It was a good stone's throw, and uphill, too. Plus Wayotel had had an injured shoulder.

"You healed yourself?" Kaiyoo asked.

Wayotel beamed. "Yes! The spell worked! I couldn't quite make the scars go away. I kept trying over and over. But the bleeding stopped and the pain was gone. And I could use my arm correctly again."

He stretched both of his dirty arms over his head, crossing them and turning them in all directions.

Kaiyoo felt awful that he had caused such pain in his friend. But he was also thankful that his power had saved him, saved them both, as Wayotel had said.

"Last night..." Kaiyoo began, shaking his head in disbelief, but he was cut off by his friend.

"It was two nights ago," Wayotel interrupted. "You've been asleep for two days."

"Really?"

"I was getting afraid you might not wake up. I was worried something had happened to you. I don't quite understand how your changing happens. I was afraid something had gone wrong."

Wayotel burst into tears. "Oh, Kaiyoo! I was so afraid you were gone too, and I was gonna be on my own. I didn't know what to do. So I just stayed, kept close, watched you for any sign you were getting better. I did the best to keep the rain off of us. It rained almost the whole time. It only just stopped this morning. I was so afraid those Nagual would find us. I didn't know what else to do."

Kaiyoo crawled over to his friend and hugged him tightly. "You did great, Wayotel. I'm proud of you. You did just great."

"It was awful," Wayotel sobbed. "I was so scared...of you! What you can change into. It is horrible. I wasn't so afraid of the river as I was that you'd kill me."

"But I didn't," Kaiyoo soothed. "I'd never hurt you, my friend. It doesn't matter whether I'm in this form or not. I saved you even though I don't remember it. We are connected, you know. You are my Tonal. I am Nahuatl now that I have changed, and when I'm older and can control it, I'll be Nihuatl to you and the rest of the world. I've felt that ever since the day Tommakee and I first came to your camp. That feeling has become stronger every day. I know you've felt it too."

Kaiyoo held his friend at arm's length so he could look into his tear-stained face. "We're in this together, to whatever end the Great Spirit has put in our path."

Wayotel nodded, his sobbing now simmered down to whimpers.

***

The sun's overhead descent into the west was well underway, and the shadows of night had already begun to lengthen. It was only a couple of days after the longest day of the year, but already the summer days were getting shorter. In their land, summer was the shortest season, and it would blend into fall in less than two full moons. The icy grip of winter held the throne for the better part of the year.

The boys' stomachs were slightly appeased once they found several handfuls of berries and a couple of unripe tree fruits. The hard green fruits were tough and bitter, but they didn't care. They hadn't wandered far from the riverbank where they had rested the

past few days, and now they were down at the water's edge. Despite the small bits of floating, burned residue, the boys each drank their fill. The water possibly tasted even more horrible than the fruit.

"Kaiyoo, what are we going to do?" whispered Wayotel.

He was just a stone's throw from returning to the whining little boy that Kaiyoo had met only a few weeks earlier. The events of the recent night had shocked Wayotel far worse than Kaiyoo.

"We need to get across this river," Kaiyoo stated. "My tribe is to the north, your people were heading toward Atolaco. If we're going to find help, it'll be that way."

The two boys looked across the rushing water. There was no way they could swim across—it was far too deep and the current was too fast. Even now, after a couple of days, the water was a murky brown topped with black, scorched bits of logs and other flotsam.

"If only we had something sharp, we could cut down a tree and float it across," Kaiyoo said, looking wistfully at the trunks around them.

"There's nothing useful around here. I've been looking around for food, but there's really nothing else," Wayotel responded. "We need to move on."

"Well we can't go back there," Kaiyoo pointed upstream. "There's nothing but destruction and danger that way."

"But heading downstream, the river will only get wider and more difficult to cross."

Kaiyoo shrugged. "You said it yourself—we can't stay here. And we can't go back toward Atolaco unless we want to run into those Nagual again. That leaves only one option."

"Do you think Atolaco was destroyed in the fire?" Wayotel's eyes dropped. It was a question that he hoped he didn't know the answer to.

Sighing, Kaiyoo put his hand on Wayotel's shoulder. "I don't see how anything could have survived that fire."

"And the Nagual?" asked Wayotel. "They were there to wipe out anyone who escaped the flames, weren't they?"

Now it was Kaiyoo's turn to reflect. "The Nagual had it all planned. Somehow they knew that the Guardians would be fighting against each other. The lightning that struck the Council Glade was no mere coincidence. That fire was designed to trap everyone, to kill us all. The Nagual were only there to hunt down any survivors."

"Do you think any of the Nihuatl survived?"

Kaiyoo closed his eyes and reached outward with his mind. He was still really just an apprentice, but he was learning to control his own powers. Doing so would help lead him to become a grown Nihuatl someday. After a few moments of intense concentration, the boy shook his head. "I can't feel any of them anymore. I don't know for sure, but I think they're all gone."

"You could tell if they were alive, right?" asked Wayotel. "You have that connection with them."

"I did have that connection," Kaiyoo whispered. "But no longer."

They were silent for a minute. Then Wayotel asked, "How far from the city do you think we are?"

"Far enough that they haven't found us in two days. The Nagual, I mean."

"Maybe they don't know we made it."

"Or they haven't searched this far yet."

Wayotel looked past his friend at the river in the distance. "The way the river was flowing that night, I'd guess we traveled at least a long day's walk. Maybe two."

They both looked back upstream, trying to imagine just how far they were from the waterfall and the city. And from where the fire had stopped burning.

Wayotel sighed. "I guess we should get going. We've been here long enough."

"Yes," Kaiyoo agreed. "Our enemies could be anywhere. We'll have to be silent."

Together, the two boys, the only living refugees of the devastation of the world's great capital city of Atolaco, noiselessly trekked through the thick foliage in the direction of the setting sun.

***

The boys covered the greatest distance in the very early mornings and as the shadows fell at twilight each evening. Fearful of being overheard by an unseen enemy, they spoke not a word except when they stopped to rest. Even then, they only whispered.

It was fairly slow going, as there was no path to follow on this side of the river. Several times they could see the wide trail on the north side of the river, though luckily there were no enemies about. Though they wanted desperately to find help, the boys had agreed that they should trust no one. Not after the betrayal that had occurred at the Guardian Council. The Dogmen weren't the only enemies in the land—they had help from dark-hearted men as well.

Constant hunger gnawed at their bellies. Wayotel was very good at finding berries and nuts for them to eat. He even located the eggs of a wild chicken. But it was never enough.

Kaiyoo, on the other hand, had the keen eyes and ears of a hunter. He could see the potential meals of game birds and small mammals, but without a weapon there was not much he could do. They couldn't even set a trap or snare because they were constantly on the move. They couldn't afford to stop for any reason.

Kaiyoo and Wayotel knew that they must cross the river to reach help from their own tribes. But not a single means of crossing presented itself. Wayotel was no better a swimmer than he was just over a month ago when they had first crossed a river on the way to Atolaco, a crossing that nearly cost them their lives. Now, downstream from the ruined city, the river was wider, and the current was even faster.

Facing possible death from exposure, starvation, and potential enemies all around them, the boys could only trust to their luck as they journeyed silently forward.

Chapter 2

They had been traveling in this silent manner for nearly four full days. The Atolaco River was always on their right, the thick forest on their left. There was no sign of friend or foe, nor was there much available food. At night, they found shelter as best as they could, huddled together for warmth.

As the sun was setting on the fourth day, its fingers of light dancing through the trees' leaves ahead of them, Kaiyoo suddenly froze, holding his palm back against Wayotel. In a flash, the two boys dropped to their knees, their bodies hidden beneath the wide fern fronds that covered much of the forest floor.

Wayotel knew immediately that Kaiyoo's excellent hearing had picked up something. He held his breath and closed his eyes, concentrating hard to pick up what his friend had heard.

Both boys listened to something moving through the underbrush ahead. It wasn't loud, but it sounded big. Kaiyoo thought he heard a voice, leading him to think it was a man rather than an animal. His eyes darted to the ground nearby looking for any sort of weapon—a rock, a stick, anything he could get his hands on quickly. He looked at Wayotel, who shook his head nervously. There was nothing around them but ferns.

Whoever—or whatever—was out there was coming closer.

The boys were almost perfectly concealed, but that wouldn't suffice if whatever it may be stumbled within 15 feet of them.

Wayotel was so flat to the ground that all he could see was his companion's ribcage. Looking up, he saw Kaiyoo lift his head slightly above the ferns. Wayotel's eyes widened in panic, and he tried to pull his friend back down by the arms. His mouth whispered "No," but it was too late—Kaiyoo had jumped to his feet.

"Tommakee!"

Wayotel was stunned to see his friend jump up and to hear his voice echo through the trees. But at hearing the name of their old traveling companion, he quickly forgot all about hiding safely along the forest floor. In a moment, he was on his feet following Kaiyoo, who had already begun bounding through the ferns.

"My boys," the old traveler beamed, hugging them tightly as they crashed into him. Tommakee nearly dropped the reins of the giant horned camel, which was looking on disinterestedly a few feet behind him. "I'm so glad to see you. I'd given up hope of ever seeing anyone from Atolaco ever again."

"So you know what happened?" Kaiyoo asked.

"Yes, I've put two and two together, as they say in my world, and guessed at the rest. I'm so glad you're alright." Tommakee put his hands on his hips and sighed, smiling. His eyes were drawn to the fading sunlight. "But it's getting dark, and we need shelter. Let's collect some wood for a fire, and you can tell me all about how you boys ended up way out here."

The two boys shared the tale of their adventures as they helped the older man gather sticks and small logs for a fire. At several points during the story, Tommakee stopped and stared and shook his head slightly in disbelief.

The bright rays of sunlight slipped behind the far-off mountains, leaving only a glowing sky and the velvety darkness slowly stretched over the treetops from the east.

"Why don't we find a place to rest so you boys can eat a little? Then I'll tell you about my escape."

"Your escape?" said Wayotel.

Tommakee nodded his head, though Yuba, the shaggy camel, just gave a disinterested grunt. "It was very close. Almost too close in fact."

He smiled, a genuine warm smile that lifted the boys' spirits. "Yuba almost didn't make it."

At that, the hairy camel ducked her head and shoved Tommakee hard in the back, nearly knocking the big man down.

"Okay, okay, so maybe Yuba was fine and I almost didn't make it. Stupid camel," he said, pushing his shoulders back against the camel's head in retaliation. "Let me tell the story, won't ya?"

***

Tommakee led them a little ways from the riverbank after filling his water skins. He liked the taste of the water as little as the boys did, but it was the only source they had at the moment.

Against a small, secluded cut in a hillside, the older man struck a small, smokeless fire. The sun had set by the time they had shared a snack of dried meat and fruit.

Yuba plopped down, legs curled beneath her shaggy body with her head lying a few feet from the fire. The two boys sat against the camel's furry side, feeling the warmth of the fire on one side and the slow, steady rise and fall of the camel's body on the other. It was the warmest they had been in days.

Poking the fire's glowing embers with a stick, Tommakee began his tale.

"You saw me as I was leaving the great village. Well, I headed back west. With midsummer's eve upon me, I knew if I was to travel to the western mountains and return before winter, I'd better get moving.

"Yuba and I set off down the trail and eventually came back up out of the river valley. The sun was nearly set and the night shadows were darkening on the earth when I noticed a strange light a bit north on the prairie, in the direction from which we had traveled if you remember. It seemed too big to be a camp, and it seemed odd for anyone to stop and camp so close to Atolaco and miss the Sun Ceremony."

The boys both nodded. Attending the Sun Ceremony was the only reason any travelers would have been there the first place.

"Then I thought that maybe someone needed help, so Yuba and I quickened our pace. But soon, we realized these Good People were far beyond needing help. The light was in fact a bonfire that was already burning itself out. I only took a few glances around to realize everyone in that traveling group had been slaughtered and all of their possessions piled and set ablaze.

"The only thing still recognizable was the clan leader's shield, which must have fallen off the pyre and rolled to the edge of the fire, where it slowly smoldered. With the fire still burning low, I knew that whoever had done this might not be too far away, and that only a large or powerful group could have wiped out an entire traveling band such as this."

"What did you do?" Wayotel asked.

Tommakee shrugged. "Yuba and I had two choices. We could either stay out on the prairie where we were conspicuous, or we could head back to the dark, dense river valley where danger could be lurking behind any tree. At least out on the prairie we would encounter anything on equal footing—nothing could ambush us.

"Well, it didn't make much sense to move until dark, so Yuba and I hunkered down a ways from the fire and tried our best to blend in with the bumps and low hills of the prairie. And it was a good thing too, because just after the moon began to rise, we began to hear the howls and snarls of great beasts, as well as the footfalls of an army of men passing not too far from us, only just to the other side of the embers from the bonfire. We waited and waited, sure they'd find us, but the luck of the gods was with us."

"You waited a long time?" Kaiyoo asked.

"Yes," Tommakee continued. "After what seemed a very long time and the night had become silent again, I peeked my head up over the prairie grasses and looked about. The moon was now four arm lengths up in the sky, and it shined down brightly, illuminating the whole world. I could easily see the bonfire's embers and even the darkness of the river valley further to our south. But there were no enemies any longer, so I dragged Yuba to her feet.

"And that's when I realized we weren't alone."

"What was it?" Kaiyoo asked, intrigued.

"There was a rear-guard only a stone's throw from me. They were also hunkered down in the tall grasses. I could see them from behind, a dozen warriors crouched with spears in hand. I squinted, peering through the moonlit grass, and saw another group further beyond, and yet another one past that one. Who knows how many groups there were between myself and Atolaco. I felt something terrible was about to happen, but there was no way I could weave my way through the thick forest amid hundreds of enemies to warn the people of the great village."

The boys just stared at the old traveler.

"About that time, I turned my head and realized Yuba had abandoned me!" Tommakee shook his head in mock disbelief. "I quickly swung my head around, looking in all directions, and then finally saw a dark blob running west away from me—and from the enemy warriors, mind you—as fast as her legs could carry her. Boys, that settled it for me that instant. I took off running after Yuba as fast as my legs could carry me!"

"Didn't the warriors hear you and Yuba?" Wayotel asked.

"You'd be surprised at how silently a camel can run when she wants to," Tommakee grinned. "Yuba didn't make a sound. Me, on the other hand, I'm not so quiet. In fact, I was pounding the ground as hard as I could to put as much distance between myself and those enemies. I was out of breath when I ran right through another encampment of enemy guards."

Both boys were wide-eyed in surprise. "What happened?" they both asked together.

Tommakee broke out in a laugh. "I must have completely surprised them, because they all fell backward, shocked and screaming in fright, as I skipped right over and past them. Now, you must realize, I was just as surprised, and it all happened so quickly, I'm not even sure I thought about what I was doing. It just happened.

"I was out of breath, as I said, my arms were sore and flapping all around. So I just started screaming at the top of my lungs, some awful war cry I never even knew I had within me. Maybe it was the moonlight shining behind me, maybe it was my crazed appearance, who knows? But it worked. The warriors all dove for cover in the tall grasses, and two seconds later I was through them and sprinting again across the prairie."

Tommakee laughed, thinking back to what that must have looked like.

"Of course, at that time, I promptly stopped screaming and just kept on running, even though my side was aching and my legs were on fire. I didn't stop until I darn near ran right into Yuba, who'd crouched down once again in the grasses and was resting quite comfortably."

***

Tommakee was chuckling again softly as he laid a pair of small logs on their fire.

"How did you and Yuba get across the river?" Wayotel asked.

"And why did you cross?" Kaiyoo followed up.

Tommakee smiled widely. "Well, my boys, that is another great story. With enemies all around us in that expanse of prairie, I knew we'd be seen at some point once the sun rose. There was just too much flat land between us and the foothills to the west. That was still many days' journey away. The only place I could think of escaping to was to risk a crossing at the river.

"I was nervous about crossing at night, especially since the storm clouds were moving in fast. And I was fearful that we'd meet more enemies in the river valley. But we had to take that chance. We couldn't wait out in the flat country where we'd be seen for sure.

"We hunkered down in the tall grasses until the thick clouds overtook the moon. That darkened everything up pretty well. Then I pulled Yuba up by the reins and we bee-lined straight for the river. By the time we made our way through the trees and down the bank, the rain had already started. At the river's edge, I tripped, almost falling over a log. It gave me a great idea."

The boys' eyes locked on Tommakee as he continued the story. "I slapped Yuba on the backside and she hopped right into the water. I followed, dragging in that log with me. I'm a pretty good swimmer you know, and Yuba can swim with the best of them. But that's a wide river, and the current is swift. I wedged myself between that floating log and Yuba the entire way across, sure to keep a tight grip on her reins and a handful of her thick fur. The log kept me afloat, and all I had to do was to kick my feet.

"As we were almost halfway across, the rain fell heavier and I could feel the river rising. The noisy current pushed us further and further downstream, even as we paddled our way across. It was a good thing there weren't any enemy warriors around, what with all of Yuba's snorting and honking and such."

The two boys shook as the great camel shuddered, sneezing and passing gas simultaneously. Her eyes didn't open even though her head flopped over. Both boys looked at each other and giggled.

"Yeah, she knows I'm talking about her, even when she's sleeping," Tommakee sighed. "Anyhow, we eventually made it across, though we were quite a ways downriver by the time Yuba pushed me up out of the water. It was a good thing we got out then, because not a minute later the whole river was thickly roiling with logs and branches, and that water surge was intense. There was a charred smell to everything, but it was too dark to see much in detail."

Tommakee poked the fire with his stick. "We managed to crawl our way up the muddy riverbank. Well, Yuba found her footing better than I did. She waited for me while I dragged myself up by long grasses and tree roots. Exhausted, we collapsed on each other in a small copse of trees that only allowed a little of the drizzle to fall on us."

***

The boys sat silently, staring into the glowing embers. No one spoke for a very long time. The only sounds were crickets and frogs out in the darkness.

Kaiyoo was the first to look up and speak. "So, where do we go from here, Tommakee?"

"I'm not really sure, boys. I only know it's dangerous to stay here, so close to Atolaco."

"But we've traveled so far from the city," Kaiyoo said earnestly. "Surely we're safe from the Nagual now."

Tommakee frowned. "I'm afraid not. Everything I've heard, every story I've been told, would lead me to believe we're in great

danger. Everyone, everywhere is in great danger. These Dogmen creatures and the dark warriors they are commanding, they're spreading like a plague from the northlands. They destroy everything they encounter. We have to keep moving. Our only chance is to find help, to find refuge in a more secure place."

"But where can we go?" Wayotel asked.

The old traveler let out a deep breath. "I have an idea. It's a dangerous idea, but not any less dangerous than staying around here. There are two places, at least according to the old legends, that the Nagual avoid."

"What are they?" the two boys said almost in unison.

"One is to the far south. The home of the Ocelotil, the Jaguar Guardians. If you remember the old stories, it was the Ocelotil who defeated the Nagual at the end of the First Age. If they were to take us in, they would be powerful allies, a fighting force that could easily match the might of this Dogman army."

"How far is it?" asked Kaiyoo. "Can we get there before we're caught?"

Tommakee stared back into the fire. "No, not likely. I've never traveled far into the southlands. Only to a few of the villages beyond the great river. This is really as far as I've ever been, following the southern bank of the river toward the west. I've heard that it's a long, long way to reach the jungles of the far south. It could take months to reach that land. The going would be slow through thickly brambling woods and swamps. No, I don't think that's the best way to take."

"What then?"

"The great western mountains," Tommakee answered slowly. "I've traveled into their foothills before. It's quite a ways, but not nearly as far as heading south. We could be there by the next full moon. There are plenty of places for us to hide out if need be—caves, ledges, ravines. The high ground is ever an advantage in a skirmish. I know of several villages where we might find help along the way, even though we might need to backtrack a bit to reach them.

"And according to the legends, the Dogmen have their own enemies, older and more powerful, who live up in the mountains themselves."

Kaiyoo stared at the old traveler. "Who are these enemies?"

Tommakee yawned. "Another tale for another night, I think. It's getting late, and we have some long days of travel ahead. We need our rest."

"I'm really worried about my family," Wayotel quietly said, looking down at his hands.

Kaiyoo thought for a minute. "Mine too. Have you had any word from them?"

Tommakee hung his head a little and paused before speaking again. "Wayotel," he began, "about your family...you see...that burning pyre I told you about?"

Wayotel's eyes began to tear up as the realization hit him. The old man clambered around the fire and put his arm around the boy.

"I'm sorry, my boy, I'm so very sorry, but...it was your grandfather's shield, the one that I saw near the fire."

Wayotel could control himself no longer. His face melted into sobs of agony as he buried himself against Tommakee's chest and shoulder.

Chapter 3

It made no sense to remain where they were, not with so many enemies around them, hidden potentially behind every boulder, tree trunk, or hill. It was a miracle they hadn't been found already. Their plan was as simple as it was dangerous. The three companions headed west toward the great mountains. Kaiyoo's tribe knew these mountains as the *Yohuali Cuautla*. Tommakee called them the "Mountains of Night," where according to legend the sun was eaten at the end of each day before being reborn in the east the following morning. The boys in their youth had been told of such legends, but now that they were headed there, they seemed more grisly and aptly fitting.

Tommakee said those mountains were supposedly haunted, that strange noises were heard in that wilderness, from the land to the waters to the sky.

He had heard from the elders in some of the local villages that those mountains were the home of huge, unfriendly beasts that could shake the ground when they walked.

Neither Kaiyoo nor Wayotel had ever seen the mountains, true mountains that rose in sharp, snowy peaks high above the plains. Tommakee in his wanderings had climbed the foothills of the *Yohuali Cuautla*, but he had never stayed longer than was necessary to trade with the few local villages. He never felt comfortable so near to the mountains. He always felt like he was being watched.

And according to the legend, the Nagual avoided the mountains because of an ancient enemy.

In all, their plan wasn't too bad. If the Dogmen weren't likely to head that way, their chances of survival increased tremendously.

***

Within a day, the Atolaco River began to angle its way more to the southwest. According to Tommakee, it would soon meet up with another river, the Misishoshai, from the north. Then the two, becoming one, would head straight many, many leagues to the southlands. Tommakee's plans were to attempt a crossing a bit beyond the rivers' convergence at a place where he knew that it widened out. The current would be stronger than ever, but the water was generally smooth.

"And I know of someone who might help us out," Tommakee said as he pulled on Yuba's reins. "If we can find her. If she's willing. If our enemy hasn't gotten to her first."

Kaiyoo looked up at the old traveler. "Who is this person? It's someone you know?"

Tommakee walked on a couple of steps silently before answering. "No, I've never actually met her. She is called Nam. It's said she's a Guardian of the river."

"Do you mean a Guardian, like the Nihuatl are guardians?" asked Wayotel.

"I don't know for sure," replied the older man. "There's really only the stories that the riverfolk tell. In the villages near the Misishoshai, it is said that a powerful creature guards and protects the river. Some say the creature is a woman, and that she is a skin-changer. Some say you can only travel south on the river by her leave. All of the stories say she is extremely dangerous."

"What do you believe?" Kaiyoo asked.

Tommakee stopped and Yuba nudged his shoulder with her snout. "I've been to many corners of this good land. I've heard many stories. I've seen many things that have come to life right out of legends. Sometimes the most fantastic creatures truly emerge from the most fantastic stories."

Tommakee began walking again. "Do I believe there's a Guardian ahead of us? If she hasn't yet been killed by the Dogman army, then I believe we are destined to find her. I only hope that we can convince her to help us cross."

Wayotel shrugged his shoulders. "We aren't really a threat to her or her river."

"Remember your teachings, my boy. Most of the Guardians I've ever heard of live solitary lives, not passing judgment on what is either deemed good or evil. They are in the world to protect. Remember the great lodge back in Atolaco? I'm sure it took the wood of hundreds, maybe thousands, of trees to construct it. Trees that were cut down and fashioned by men. Trees that some Guardian, great or small, had undoubtedly protected. The great lodge wasn't built for an evil purpose, nor by evil men. But to one of the lesser Guardian spirits, it didn't matter. The trees were still cut down."

They all walked on in silence for a bit. Overhead, the sky was mostly gray. It was almost midday, but the sun's rays were already fighting to break through the gathering clouds.

Tommakee looked into the boys' eyes. "You must remember we're now heading into lands where I've never been. I've only ever been to the northern foothills of the Mountains of Night. When we cross the great river this far south, we will be in unfamiliar territory."

***

Two days later, traveling ever so slightly downhill and trudging through moist, soft ground, they could hear the sound of the convergence of the rivers before they could actually see them.

The treeline ended a couple of dozen feet before the land dropped steeply to the river itself. Looking north, the boys could see where the two rivers met in the distance. Dozens of charred logs had piled up at the vertex of the two rivers churning the water's surface.

Wayotel was the first to speak. "It's much wider here. No way I could get across that on my own."

The trees on the opposite shore looked rather small from where they stood. The river was as wide as many of the lakes the boys had seen. Kaiyoo knew he couldn't throw a stone a dozen times and hit land on the opposite side. Perhaps it would even take a couple dozen. Good, hard throws using all his strength.

Tommakee's eyes slowly searched up and down the banks. He pointed south. "Let's keep following the river. I'm thinking we'll find her in this direction."

***

It began drizzling as they walked along the soft, red earth above the riverbank. Deep footprints were left behind them. They had traveled just far enough to leave the water's loud turbulence at the log deadlock when Tommakee spotted something floating in the middle of the river.

Yuba whined and pulled her reins back in the direction of the treeline. Both boys saw the object in the water at the same time, and their eyes widened in fear. They both began backing up until Tommakee stopped them.

"Whoa there, guys," the old man chided them and the camel, holding firm to the straps. "Everybody stand still. Don't move."

Kaiyoo had seen turtles before. He and the other children of his village used to catch them in streams, fascinated by these flexible little creatures that lived within such a hard exterior. The biggest turtles they had found, those a couple of hands wide, would be taken back to the village to make a hearty soup.

At the moment, Kaiyoo was regretting every bowl of turtle soup he'd ever eaten.

The curved, brownish-green shell quickly approached the river's edge directly in front of them. Raindrops bounced off of the smooth shell, which Tommakee estimated to be about eight feet across.

About 20 feet from the riverbank, the turtle's great head rose up out of the water. Its neck, striped with green, brown, and tan, was easily as long as one of Yuba's legs. Above and behind its black eyes was a red oval marking. The turtle blinked, then opened its great beak and took air. Then it submerged. Only a handful of bubbles remained, momentarily breaking the surface.

That was enough for the camel. Yuba blared a high-pitched honking noise and ripped the reins free from Tommakee's hand. She bolted for the safety of the trees. The boys looked at Tommakee, who stood fast upon the ground. He swallowed hard, unsure of what would happen next.

Then the river's surface broke in a splash of water.

Where the gigantic turtle had been only moments ago was now a woman, swimming easily in the murky water. She was only discernible from the shoulders up. Specs of mud and flotsam from the river clung to her short tan hair and oval-shaped face.

She could have been 50 years old or 150. All three of the travelers knew she must have been far older than that. And yet she was beautiful in her own natural way. Her skin was a mottled pattern of brown and green shapes that resembled softened rectangles and trapezoids. Her ears were small and flat against the sides of her head, and hanging from them were red, oval pendants.

To Tommakee's mind, she resembled a mermaid, though she was anything but slim and alluring as mermaids were always described.

"You are strangers here," she said in a calm and yet authoritative tone.

"We are looking for Nam," Tommakee said pleasantly. He pointed at the opposite shore, which now seemed awfully far away. "We are humble travelers, looking for help to get across. We know that none should pass this river without her leave."

The woman effortlessly swam to the bank, unimpeded by the strong current around her.

"Turn your eyes away, boys," Tommakee instructed, as it became clear she was going to exit the water without any clothing on herself. The two boys sat on the ground and faced back toward the forest. Neither looked toward the river as the woman walked right up out of the water and up the steep riverbank.

Tommakee dropped to one knee and bowed his head, lowering his eyes to the ground in a sign of respect. He held his palms upward to show they had come in peace.

Patiently, he waited for her to speak. Tommakee raised his head when she gently touched him on the shoulder. He stood, and yet he still had to look further up because she was easily a head taller than him. The rain had cleared her face and hair of the splatters of river mud. She had somehow covered herself in a dark green wrap that was tied around her neck and waist, flowing almost to her ankles.

"I am Nam. Welcome to River Crossing."

***

Despite the rain that was now steadily falling, Nam's green garment seemed completely dry. As she walked, this wrap flowed around her large and muscular body, though all three travelers could discern she was not fat in any way.

Her gigantic, bare feet left hardly a mark upon the muddy ground as she led them toward a stone outcropping a short distance from the river. Wayotel thought it looked like a pile of huge flat boulders that some giant had set in place. In seconds they had all passed through an opening in the rocks and were inside. Only Yuba remained out in the rain, slowly pacing among the nearby trees.

Pleasantly surprised by the cave's expansive interior, Tommakee and the boys were relieved to be out of the rain.

Nam raised her arms, and her fingers dragged along the ceiling of the cave. Immediately, a greenish glow radiated from the trails her fingers had made until the entire chamber was alighted. It wasn't a huge cavern, maybe 20 feet across, guessed Tommakee. On the smooth walls were brightly colored paintings of simple scenes—rivers, animals, and turtles. Many, many turtles, of all sizes and shapes and colors. There was no furniture, only flat areas of stone raised at different heights.

Nam sat down on one of these flat surfaces and eyed the three newcomers, who promptly sat down at her feet. When she spoke, her voice was soft and slow.

"You three do make an unusual company, yes indeed. I don't have anything but shelter to offer you. It's too bad. You look like you've walked instead of eaten in days. You could all use a little fattening-up, I'd say."

The old man stated kindly, "Wise mother, you speak as if you were expecting us.

I'm guessing we're not the only ones to have been here recently."

Nam gently turned her hands over and over again, as if examining her skin. "There were dark men here. Two days ago. They mistook me for a defenseless old woman." Nam absently waved her wrinkled hand back toward the cave's entrance. "I must be getting old. One of them actually managed to escape." She smiled, chuckling. "Of course, he'll find life difficult with only one hand."

"I can only imagine their surprise," answered Tommakee with a brief chuckle of his own. The two boys simply sat still and listened to the exchange between the adults.

Nam stared deeply at them one by one. "No, it wasn't me they'd come for. They were here, looking for you."

"How would they know anything about us, wise mother?" asked Kaiyoo.

Nam reached into a satchel lying near where she was sitting and then uncurled her hand. In it were three small chunks of wood held together by some sort of thin animal sinew. Two of the chunks were smaller and of a dark wood. The third was bigger and made of a lighter colored wood. All three of the wooden pieces were slashed diagonally from the upper left to lower right corner with a cut that had been stained red.

"They're hunting you."

***

By the light of the cave's green glow, Tommakee shared their tale and described why they needed to reach the safety of the river's far shore.

"So, the Nagual have come again, have they?" Nam sighed. "I had feared as much. We're coming to the end of this age of the world. The Nagual and their master will try their best to cover the land in darkness."

"I was there, you know," Nam continued, nodding to the travelers. "Long, long ago, at the end of the world's First Age. The river and the land were very different then, but the battle was still the same. So much of it happened far to the south. That was where I used to protect this great river. Once they were defeated, I came here."

She smiled, a beautiful, radiant smile that lit up her face even in the dim glow of the cave's ceiling. "I like it here. Two rivers that join into one. A place of beauty, a place of power. The perfect place for Nam."

She returned to her serious visage. "I will live on, as I always have, no matter what these Nagual do to the rest of the world. If the great Guardians can be assembled in time, I will join with them. If not," she shrugged, "I will stay here and protect this river to the last of my power."

The boys squirmed uneasily on the hard stone floor. It was very difficult to remain still and silent for such a long time. Nam turned her attention to them.

"That amulet you wear," she said, looking at Kaiyoo. "You are now Nahuatl. Son of a Guardian, I see. I sense great power in you. I could feel your approach these past few days, like ripples on calm water. That was how I knew to expect you.

"Just like the ancient legends. The two of you—the brothers who will unite the last of the great Guardians in the world."

Wayotel looked at Kaiyoo and then up at Nam, stuttering, "We are not of the same tribe, honored mother."

A smile, true and wide lit up Nam's face. She laughed and was quickly joined by Tommakee. The Guardian, still pleased, said, "You are not brothers of the blood. You are brothers of the spirit."

Pointing at Kaiyoo, Nam said, "You are young, but I can see you'll be a powerful Nihuatl some day. Why else would the enemy be hunting you? Why else would he want you destroyed?"

"And you," Nam said, pointing at Wayotel, "are obviously his Tonal. Your magical powers are developing, more and more each day. Am I not right?"

The two boys looked at each other, giving small smirks.

"We could share more stories about the ancient legends and the mystic deeds of heroic brothers all night, but I sense you need to leave this great river valley. Those dark men I dispatched not too long ago were only a scouting party. I have no doubt a larger force will return here, and in the not too distant future."

"Will you help us, wise one? Can you get us quickly across the river?" Tommakee asked as they all waited in anticipation.

"You are not just escaping the ruins of the Guardian city. Nor are you fleeing the horrible darkness that is filling the land. You have become a part of the fabric of legend itself. You are writing yourselves into tales that will be told for a millennium. Seeing you here, hearing your tale, knowing your purpose—of course I will help you on your way. It is my honor to stand once more against the lord of the underworld and his dark minions."

Nam nodded her head slowly and then spoke. "We can go at any time. I think you'll only need to go round-up your beast."

47

***

"Must it always rain whenever we want to cross a river?" complained Wayotel as they emerged from Nam's cave. He vividly remembered the trouble they had on their journey to Atolaco. He had almost drowned when their raft capsized.

"Let's just be thankful our gracious host is willing to take us across," Tommakee replied. He had managed to drag Yuba back out of the treeline and down to the shore. The river seemed to swell with the pouring rain. "We wouldn't get very far trying to swim it ourselves."

Nam smiled and stroked the camel's face gently. Then she scratched its ears. She was tall enough to actually look down into Yuba's eyes. "You're just a tasty tidbit, aren't you? It's a good thing your master is here. If you'd come alone down to my waters for a drink, I think you'd be joining me for dinner." Yuba squinted her eyes at the woman as if knowing exactly what was on the Guardian's mind. But the camel didn't dare pull away, not with her this close.

The Guardian turned to Tommakee. "Your beast is plenty nervous around me. It would be best if I led her across while I'm in human form. I don't think she'd trust me otherwise."

The traveler agreed. "We'll need to cross in two trips to save time. Kaiyoo, you go first with Yuba. Then Wayotel and I will make the second trip."

Kaiyoo was reluctant to part with the other two, but what Tommakee said made sense. Slipping down the embankment, Kaiyoo followed Nam, who was leading Yuba. Tommakee had to give the camel a good slap on the rear flank to get her moving, and a second later all three were in the deep, brown water.

Kaiyoo hooked his arm around Yuba's neck and clung closely to her, keeping his head up above the water. Nam swam straight across the current with a single strong-arm stroke, all the while pulling on the camel's reins. Despite the rain and the pressure of the fast water around them, Kaiyoo felt completely relaxed as the Guardian led them across.

Before he knew it, Kaiyoo and Yuba were led right up the riverbank. Nam's footing was perfect as before, despite the rainwater streaming down the soil and turning everything to slippery mud.

Taking the reins, Kaiyoo thanked the woman and then led the camel away from the steep embankment. Nam smiled and carefully walked back into the water.

***

Kaiyoo heard the Nagual before he saw it.

Nam was just over halfway back when the attack came from the forest behind Tommakee and Wayotel. Fierce war cries echoed through the trees as more than a dozen human warriors charged forth. They were clothed in all black skins and carried long spears. Their faces were as wild as their hair and beards.

And they were led by a savage Dogman, roaring loudly and sprinting powerfully toward Tommakee and Wayotel on all four legs.

Kaiyoo shouted, but his voice was drowned out by the rain, which was now heavily pouring down around them. He quickly scrambled up a nearby slope that looked over the river so he could see better.

On the other side of the river, Tommakee heard the war cries behind him, and he reacted before he had time to even think. "Jump, boy! Jump for your life!" he yelled, actually pushing a surprised Wayotel into the river before the boy could even decide to jump himself. Tommakee leapt in, right on the boy's heels.

Once Tommakee surfaced, it took him only a moment to locate Wayotel, who of course had bobbed back up flailing his arms and struggling to keep his head above water. The old traveler swam to him, aided by the strong current. They had already floated quite a distance from where they had jumped in, to the dismay of their attackers.

Nam dipped beneath the surface and emerged in her Guardian form. The great turtle wasted no time in darting downstream to catch up with the two. Within seconds, both Tommakee and Wayotel were lifted right out of the water on the turtle's shell.

Tommakee grabbed hold of the boy's sleeve with one hand and the edge of the shell with the other. He sputtered, "Grab the edge so you don't slip off." Wayotel, coughing and spitting out river water, did as he was instructed, and soon they were out of spear range and headed for the opposite shore.

***

The Nagual skidded to a halt at the riverbank, claws digging into the soft soil. It savagely looked at the prey that had barely escaped its clutches. It followed down the riverbank for a brief period until it saw the Guardian rescue the two humans. Then the Dogman turned back and stood up on its hind legs. It growled a command at the dark warriors, pointing first at the forest and then at the river.

Driving their spears into the now muddy ground, the warriors began scavenging around the edge of the forest while the Nagual turned back to stare across the river.

Within minutes, the dark men began dragging thick logs to the river's edge.

***

To Kaiyoo, it seemed an eternity watching and waiting as his friends came across as his enemies attempted to find a way to pursue them. Already, the dark men were assembling crude rafts to follow the three. The last of them had finished dragging logs out of the forest while others were tying them tightly together. As Kaiyoo watched, the first raft slid down the riverbank and into the water with two evil men upon it. The other crudely built log rafts soon joined the hunt.

In actuality, Nam in her Guardian form could swim twice as fast as in her human form, even as she carried the two travelers on her back. Yet she was careful to ensure they wouldn't fall off into the swelling river. She reached the shore just as the last of the enemy rafts entered in the water.

The turtle's shell slipped right up against the bank so that Tommakee and Wayotel could slide right off onto the shore. Kaiyoo had come down and helped pull his two companions up away from the river. Once up on solid ground, the three looked down at the Guardian.

"You go, and may the Great Spirit look kindly on your journey," Nam said in her slow, deep voice. She looked away from the three travelers. "I'll deal with them."

Nam turned her mighty head back toward the opposite shore. It took her no time at all to cross.

Tommakee tugged at the two boys. "Let's get going."

"No, wait," Kaiyoo said. "I want to see this."

From atop the rise, the three stopped to watch. The distance and the heavy downpour did little to diminish the battle that was over very quickly. Nam, in her Guardian form, was terrible to behold. The great turtle approached the first rafts, her hard shell repelling the warriors' spears. Her beak rose up and tore a chunk right out of the nearest log, flipping the raft end over end. The second raft capsized moments later, followed soon after by all of the rest.

The cries of the evil warriors died out quickly as they were dragged to a horrible death beneath the river's surface.

Atop the riverbank, the Dogman paced back and forth on its two hind legs, fiercely snarling at the destructive scene below. It had meant to jump aboard the last raft, but the sight of the powerful Guardian gave it enough of a pause, a choice that undoubtedly saved its life.

Having dispatched all of the warriors, Nam casually swam toward the Dogman. She stopped just 10 feet from the edge of the water, a distance the Nagual could easily leap. Tommakee and the boys would never see the smile that formed on the turtle's beaked mouth or hear the chomping clicks she made, challenging the Nagual to jump on in and battle.

The Dogman, however, knew it was bested at the moment. Its eyes glowed an evil yellow, and it gave one last sharp-toothed roar across the river and up into the sky before it dropped to all fours and sprinted back into the forest.

The two boys shivered, and not just from the cold of the river and the falling rain. The Nagual's roar was terrifying enough, even without the horrible memories they had from the slaughter of the Guardians at Atolaco only a few weeks ago and their own encounter with two deadly Dogmen.

"Now we need to go," Tommakee said urgently. "They'll soon be back with a greater force. And I'm sure they'll look for a safer place to cross, far away from her."

Chapter 4

Thick clouds continued to hide the sun for the better part of the next week. It drizzled or outright rained for most of that time. But for as long as they continued through the wide expanse of forest, the daytime temperature was at least tolerable and there was little wind.

They were able to find plenty of food each day. The summer would soon come to an end and the many wild plants had already been giving up their bountiful foodstuffs. All three knew to dig up the roots and tubers of many plants, finding them moist and delicious. The boys laughed when Tommakee called the orange ones *karruts* and the brown ones *taters*. They often asked him about his homeland, where he must have learned such an unusual language, but the old man would just smile and wave his hand, telling them that was a long story for another day.

Being on the move constantly, all three missed having meat. The boys had taken to sharpening small throwing spears whenever they stopped for a break. A couple of times they had thrown at rabbits or plump birds, but they had yet to hit the mark. Secretly, Tommakee hoped the two boys wouldn't need to use such skills in a battle if their lives depended on it.

Most of all, Kaiyoo missed having a big fire at night. The last time the three traveled together, they'd had a great time. Tommakee would tell stories, they ate from the great supply of dried meat from Wayotel's tribe, and the boys played and sang around the fire. At night, they had great warmth, as even after the warmest days the nights could be frigid.

Now, they were afraid to light anything but the smallest of fires for fear of attracting the wrong type of attention. Many nights they simply did without a fire, especially if they were out in the open at all. The evil warriors of Xoloctal, the Dogmen, and perhaps even worse things could be out hunting at night.

The nights were getting colder. They could tell in even just the few weeks since they joined up. Now that the festival of the sun was over, marking the midpoint of their land's short summer season, every day and every night would lead them closer to the long, dark winter months.

Tommakee worried about more than just fleeing their enemy. At some point he knew they would have to begin thinking about winter survival. And winter would come much faster as they traveled up into the mountains.

Each passing day led them past more and more trees whose leaves were already changing colors, transforming the primeval forest from the sea of green to an explosion of fiery reds, waves of amber and orange, and sparkles of gold.

It was also getting steadily cooler during the day as they slowly made the climb up into the higher elevations, the foothills rising before the great western mountains. Neither boy had been wearing much in the way of clothing when they'd barely escaped the slaughter back in Atolaco. Luckily for them, Tommakee kept extra clothing in the pack tied to Yuba's back. Both Kaiyoo and Wayotel were already arrayed in one of the bigger man's long-sleeve shirts that draped loosely around the boys' slim figures.

The days were generally peaceful as they marched on. They saw not a soul in this wilderness. It was even rare to see any animals, and that worried Tommakee far more than he allowed himself to say in front of the boys. In fact, the wildlife they saw the most were the flocks of birds overhead, flying south to escape the oncoming winter. That bothered Tommakee. Normally the birds didn't start seriously heading south for another month at least. And the forest creatures? They too were holing themselves up prematurely.

Winter was coming, as it always did. Only this year, everything in nature pointed to it coming early.

***

The day after the full moon, which in this season was coincidentally called by Wayotel's tribe the "journey moon," and one full month since Atolaco was destroyed in flame, the three travelers saw the distant mountain peaks for the first time. They had climbed up an embankment to a rocky outcropping bare of trees. Awed by the sight, the two boys just stood and stared, speechless. Their eyes traveled the faint, jagged lines of the ridge high above them, back and forth from one edge of the treeline to the other.

Having seen the mountains himself many times, both in this world and in his past life, Tommakee took just a moment to be impressed once again at the geological wonder of nature before plopping down to rest on the rocky ledge. Yuba was unimpressed, instead turning her head away to stare absentmindedly back toward the far-stretching woodlands below.

While the boys continued to marvel at the mountains, Tommakee had the chance to reflect on his rather extensive knowledge of the Earth's last glacial period and the ending of that ice age. He was a trained paleogeologist, at least in his life before coming to this world.

While the reality of the world around him here differed slightly from what he had learned in his studies and research, he still clearly understood that he had traveled back in time roughly 10,000 years. It was still the Earth. It fit paleontologists' descriptions and proved their theories. And he was actually here to see it, to experience it himself.

That was a small consolation, considering there was no way back to his former life.

He knew that just after the Wisconsin glacial episode, a period of warming had occurred before the "little ice age" plummeted North America back into the deep freeze. His mind often repeated the question, *Is this the world before or after the little ice age?*

No one really knew why the little ice age, or *Younger Dryas* period, occurred. Tommakee knew there had been many theories. Most indicated a collapse of the North

American ice sheets would have caused such a drastic drop in temperatures. Some scientists thought the jet stream had shifted. Others theorized an influx of fresh water that altered the North Atlantic salinity levels. However, no geological evidence had been found in Tommakee's time period to prove such claims.

Tommakee believed, as did many other scientists and historians of his day, that only some random component such as an extraterrestrial impact could have altered the climate so quickly and so harshly. But again, there had never been any archaeological evidence found of meteors, asteroids, or comets hitting the earth at that point in history. Generally, a pretty big hole would suffice, but no known craters could be linked through carbon dating to this particular time period.

That was another thing that bothered Tommakee. He had been in this world for more than 20 years, and he had seen very little change. The seasons, brutal as they were, stayed the same. The people stayed the same. The wildlife stayed the same. Even the prehistoric and mythological beasts, once you became accustomed to their presence in the world, stayed the same. Everything was the same until this year. Now the world was in turmoil. Tommakee could feel it in the earth.

He could smell it on the air. He could see it in the way life was fleeing or being extinguished.

The world around them was changing, and not in a good way.

Tommakee could feel they were all on the verge of some great cataclysmic event. Perhaps, this was even the mysterious event that would usher in the *Younger Dryas*, the "little ice age," as it was commonly referred to. His mind again returned to that question, *is this the world before or after the little ice age?* Then a newer question started to formulate. *If we're headed for the little ice age, what will be the cause of it?*

If some great impact was indeed inching its way toward them, and if it indeed was the cause of the "little ice age"—the mass extinction of the North American megafauna and the wiping out of the early human Clovis culture—then such an event would be potentially devastating to the entire continent. It would be something that happened abruptly.

There would be no escape for anyone.

And yet, despite these feelings of impending doom, nothing except an army of mythological monsters seemed destined to attempt destroying the world.

"Tommakee?" Wayotel said, pulling the older man back to the present moment. Tommakee had been staring out at the sun already well into its rapid descent toward the distant mountain peaks that were just visible beyond the little valley they were crossing. He had shivered, partly from the dropping temperature and partly from his cold thoughts.

The traveler smiled gently. "Let's get moving."

***

The climb became noticeably steeper as the thick oak forests changed to more evenly spread pines and aspens. In many places, these taller and thinner trees opened up the forest floor and balanced out their travel. The golden leaves of the aspens danced and sang in the cold winds that were now constantly nibbling the skin as they hiked into higher elevations.

Luckily there were a few extra skins and furs rolled up in the packs strapped to Yuba's back. The travelers started by each draping a layer of furs over their upper torso. Tommakee took it upon himself to start to stitch these skins and furs into wearable clothing when they stopped at the end of each day. In a few days time, both Kaiyoo and Wayotel were wearing fur-lined shirts that were an improvement over the thinner, oversized ones they had been wearing. They weren't great, but they did protect the skin a little better than what they had. Tommakee didn't need any additional clothing at the moment.

They did see signs of wild game again, but they had no time to fashion tools or hunt. It was too bad, because some fresh meat would be welcomed after eating nothing but vegetation for the past few weeks. And Tommakee had nothing left to stitch together into warmer clothing. The scraps that had been left over were sewn into quivers to hold the boys' throwing spears.

There was an uneasy silence around them, save for the wind at the treetops. They felt like they were being watched, and they believed they were being followed. Even stopping in the evenings became uncomfortable.

Kaiyoo had no more dream visions, but that didn't stop him from thinking deeply about the battle he believed he had witnessed in his mind. He hadn't shared that vision with either Wayotel or Tommakee. *The Concua Cahuayoh, the black monster of the darkest legends...could it be real? Could it really be here in the world? What could defeat it?*

***

There was at least a little warning before the next attack came.

Hiking up a fairly steep incline along a naturally treeless gully, the travelers heard the unmistakable barking howls of at least two Dogmen communicating to each other not too far in the distance.

The boys wanted to freeze and just hope the monsters would pass them by somewhere at the lower elevations. Tommakee knew better. The Nagual's sense of smell was as good as any wolf in the wild. Even if the Dogmen hadn't tracked them all the way from the river crossing, they would soon find their scent.

"Run!" Tommakee commanded quietly through his gritted teeth, and no one hesitated.

The three ran as fast as their legs could take them. Even up these steep hills with uneven footing, Yuba managed to keep pace, though the camel would have easily outdistanced the humans had they been racing on flat ground.

The distant growls were closer now, even though the Dogmen were still out of sight. Howls answered from the left and the right.

Tommakee was tiring quickly, and he knew he only had a few more minutes at the most before he would be wiped out. Already his heart was pounding in his chest and sweat was pouring down his face. He would have to make a stand soon if he was to give the boys any sort of chance of escape.

And then suddenly the first enemy was upon them, just below as it stepped into the open bottom of the gully. Its deep roar made all three travelers look back down the hill. The Dogman snarled and shook its head, spittle flying from its jaws.

The old guide knew this was the time. He slapped Yuba on the rear flank yelling, "Hai!" to send the camel up after the two boys.

Tommakee faced the Nagual, his staff in his hands. The staff had seen action many times in the past, most recently at the battle in Kayioo's village, now more than two months ago. One end of the staff was a burnished knob, solid like a hammer. The other end was sharpened to a point.

Then a second Nagual stepped into the gully from the left side and joined its counterpart. Tommakee sighed. *Of course*, he thought sarcastically, *they'd have to attack together. I couldn't be allowed to fight one at a time. Well, maybe I can at least give the boys more time to find shelter, help, something.*

Sensing their fatigued prey ahead, the Dogmen stood up on their hind legs and confidently strode up the hill, one just ahead of the other, all the while smiling in an evil manner.

***

Yuba had sprinted up just past both boys when she stopped suddenly. Her ears twitched, and then she sidestepped a few feet into the trees along the side of the gully.

Wayotel, who was several feet ahead of Kaiyoo, felt the ground shaking. He looked up, past where the horned camel had moved out of the path. An avalanche of logs was tumbling down the gully with alarming speed toward the spot where they were standing.

"Watch out!" Wayotel yelled as loudly as he could as he sprinted for the treeline. Kaiyoo followed suit, as he heard a rumble like thunder.

Tommakee had just enough time to look uphill toward the boys and then dive for the safety of a large evergreen's trunk. A second later, and only a few feet to the side, the barrage of thick logs accelerated down the hillside.

The lead Dogman's golden eyes widened in surprise, and it jerked to a sudden halt. Nimbly, this first one leapt high up over the first barreling log. But there was no way it could avoid them all.

After managing to get over two more, the Dogman's black rear feet caught the rolling edge of another timber and it went down to the flattened earth. In a moment, the remainder of the rolling logs slammed into both monsters' bodies, catching up the Dogmen and dragging the creatures down the hill. Dozens of logs, most of them two to three feet in diameter, smashed through everything in their path, crushing the undergrowth and uprooting smaller saplings.

A cloud of dust rose up, obliterating the boy's view of the scene below. Only after a bit did the loud crashing finally cease as the avalanche found its final resting place below. The boys skittered along the scuffed ground to help Tommakee to his feet.

Wayotel was still in shock. "Wha-wha-what was that?"

"I don't care, as long as it saved our hides," Tommakee replied, still trying to catch his breath. The dusty air only made his exasperation from the uphill race worse. "But I think we should keep going. Quickly."

"Don't you think those Nagual are dead?" Kaiyoo asked incredulously. "There's no way anything could have survived that."

Tommakee sputtered between gasps. "I don't know. Those creatures are...nearly indestructible. And even if they were killed below...there's at least one more out there...maybe more. You know when there's

one...we should always expect more. Either way...we can't stay here."

Wayotel looked around him and back up the steep hill. "So where did those logs come from?"

***

Scrambling quickly up the gully, the travelers found the source of the avalanche. There was clear evidence that the huge pile of logs had rested in deep ruts in the ground, and a thick log linchpin had been keeping them in place. They rested as they examined where the stockpile had been. Yuba was the only one who wasn't breathless. She just glanced around the world as disinterested as ever.

"A trap," Kaiyoo managed to say despite being winded.

Tommakee had his hands on his hips and was nearly doubled over gasping for air. "More likely...a defense. I think." He picked up the linchpin, examined it, and then stammered, "Someone...must have...just set these loose. That someone...is probably still right around here. There are bigger questions, like...were they trying to wipe us out...or wipe out the Dogmen...or just wipe us all out together?"

"Why would someone want to kill us? We're harmless." Wayotel asked, also just trying to catch his breath.

"Because you're strangers," a voice answered from above them, in a matter-of-fact voice. "We don't take any chances with strangers."

Startled, they all looked further up the hill and saw a boy smiling down at them.

The boy looked a little older and taller than Kaiyoo, though it was tough to judge him accurately since he was standing quite a bit higher than them. He had wide shoulders and a fairly broad chest. And his height was deceiving because his legs looked rather short and stocky—his upper body was a disproportionate size compared to his lower body.

He had pitch-black hair, pulled back and tied in a short tail, with very dark skin, much darker than any of the three travelers. He wore a long-sleeved black leather shirt with a string of sparkling, brightly polished blue and creamy colored gems around his thick neck. He wore loose, black leather pants that ended just barely above his knees. All of his clothing was trimmed with frills, giving him a fuzzy, hairy appearance.

But probably the most distinct feature of the boy was his teeth. When he spoke, the three travelers saw his front two upper teeth were wider and longer than the rest, protruding almost to his bottom lip even when his mouth was wide open. Tommakee noticed that these gave the boy a lisp when he talked.

"What were those things?" the dark skinned boy asked.

"You've never seen one before?"

"No. I could just see they were coming after you and you were running like scared rabbits. They looked like something from a nightmare."

"From the very worst nightmares," Tommakee agreed. "In the old language, they're called Nagual, evil servants of Xoloctal, the ruler of the netherworld. The Nagual were once evil men, but they were ruined even further by the darkest magic, caught between the human and canine forms."

"You saw we were running like scared rabbits and you still sent the logs down at us?" Kaiyoo asked.

The boy shrugged, smiling. "Oh yes, sorry about that. No hard feelings, huh? We aren't used to strangers in our land. I was already releasing the trap when I realized you and the monsters weren't all evil together. Good thing you've got quick feet, huh!"

Yuba gave a grunt, and Tommakee nodded in agreement.

"My name is Onomineese. But everyone just calls me Ono, everybody but my mother that is. My people, the Ahuizotl, live in this land." He pointed at the linchpin still in Tommakee's hands. "We have many traps all over to keep our enemies away. A trap, a defense, it's all the same to us. You look like you could use help, after what you've been through. Come with me—our village isn't far from here. But we should hurry—night's coming and the cold is setting in."

"And there are more of those Nagual still out here somewhere," Tommakee said, looking back down the steep hill to where the logs were jammed far below. It was still far too clouded with dust to see anything accurately, but he didn't like the way he felt. The Dogmen had found them once, and pretty easily, all things considered. How long would it be before more of Xoloctal's evil minions caught up with them?

"Yes," Ono said. "I need to tell the captain about all of this."

***

They followed Onomineese upward for quite some time until the great hill finally crested. The temperature slowly dropped, coinciding with the complete change from deciduous trees to thick, green firs. Ono didn't seem to notice the cold as much as the three travelers, who had been wearing only limited lighter clothing after so much time in the warm valley around Atolaco. Even beneath the new shirts Tommakee made them, the boys' skin was still covered in goosebumps. Every few minutes one of them had a mighty shiver.

Their descent back down into the valley was much easier although steep, and Tommakee had to slow his pace so that Yuba wouldn't drag them down and slip on the pine needles and loose dirt.

Kaiyoo noticed they were following a rough trail that snaked back and forth as it descended through the forest. It must indeed be a deep valley, as they had climbed quite high on the other side of that first foothill. Onomineese had called it "the slope," sharing that the hill they had climbed, and that they had almost died upon, was the easiest way into their valley.

"Really, it's the only safe way," Ono said. "There are all sorts of pitfalls, brambles, brush piles, and traps that you can't even imagine around the top of the valley."

"Your tribe really doesn't trust strangers, huh?" Kaiyoo asked.

Ono nodded. "We really don't get any strangers here. If someone shows up in our valley that we don't know, well, it's hard to trust that they're here on a friendly purpose."

Normally, Ono shared, there wasn't much danger coming from the relatively uninhabited woods below. But with the darkening times lately, they had doubled the guard at the top of "the slope" to watch for strangers.

"We could see you from quite a ways," their new guide said as they ducked beneath the wide boughs of a tall fir. "My little cousin was perched up at the top of our lookout tree. As you were running up 'the slope' toward us, we decided to spring the trap. I sent him on ahead of us to the village to let them know what happened. The captain needed to know about those creatures."

At just that moment, they heard a shrill whistle. It was intended to sound like a bird call, but both boys recognized it as a warning. Every tribe had their own means of emergency communication.

Onomineese returned the call and from out of nowhere a trio of warriors stepped out of the brush. All three were alike to Ono in appearance, though they were bigger, more muscular, and wore thick, bushy black beards that mostly covered their faces. They carried thick, sharpened spears that were longer than the three men were tall.

Ono and the Ahuizotl warriors spoke in their own language for a few seconds, and then the three warriors passed on up the path. Kaiyoo noticed they shared the same wide, blunt front teeth as Onomineese.

"They're taking my place on lookout," Ono explained. "Usually 'the slope' is only watched by young pups like myself. But with your arrival, and those 'things' chasing you, the tribe will want some of our hardened warriors there instead."

Wayotel thought the three warriors who had passed them seemed more like big shaggy, blubbery buffalo than hardened warriors. If those were the Ahuizotl's hardened warriors, they might all be in trouble if the Nagual found them.

"If the Nagual gather and charge up the slope, how will your warriors defend themselves?" asked Kaiyoo. "The Nagual are monstrous killers."

Ono just waved a hand. "Not to worry. You only saw one of our traps. 'The slope' has many more defenses as you call them.

"No one's ever attacked us, not as long as I've been alive. I can't say that I've ever heard of any stories where anyone's even made it past our traps and entered the valley at all. Not without being invited, anyway."

They were all waved on by Onomineese, so they continued down the trail. Both boys gave another shiver as the afternoon slipped down into the colorful skies of early evening.

It won't be long until the next season, thought Kaiyoo. Already the tree leaves on the slopes of these lower elevations were starting to change color. And the nights were getting progressively cooler. Soon the ponds and slower creeks will be frozen in the mornings. And the snow will begin to fall.

***

They all saw the flicker of lights between the trees just before the trail widened its way out of the forest.

Tommakee was as amazed at the sight as the two boys were. A broad, calm lake glistened in the last of the sun's rays, just as it was dipping below the mountain peaks far to the west.

Despite his extensive travel all over this world, he had never imagined anything to match the village below. In his own world, lakefront property was a valued commodity. But the homes of this village weren't stationed on the shores. The Ahuizotl built their lodges right in the water, right out in the middle of the lake.

Each lodge was a miracle in engineering. Long and low with permanent walls and roofs made of interlocking timbers, each lodge sat atop small islands of mounded rock and log. A few narrow bridges of rope and flattened boards connected the lodges. From their vantage point still slightly above the lake, the village resembled a series of concentric circles, wheels within wheels. Four wheels in all.

Just like the city of Atlantis, thought Tommakee as he gazed at this primitive fortress city that seemed a counterpart to that ancient myth. *And it will someday join Atlantis in being obliterated and disappearing into history.*

Ono pointed far past the many lodges to the southwestern side of the flooding. There a rim of thick logs formed the boundary of the lake. "It's not really a lake, not a real lake anyway. We call it a flooding. Our ancestors dammed up the river. You can see it over at the far side of the village."

"What's beyond the dam?" asked Tommakee.

"Oh, the river continues on down the valley as it winds through the hills. I can't really say much after that. I've only ever been a little ways down that direction. Can't really say I'm much interested either, since everything we could ever want is right here around us!"

The lights were small fires set in deep bowls, which were in turn set in the water of the flooding. They cast a soft, flickering illumination all around the village. In a couple of places, wider fire bowls were burning away.

"How deep is the water?"

"Oh, I can swim all the way to the bottom in a few seconds. At its deepest, I'd say, oh, three times my height." Ono held his hand up just above his head and thought hard. "Maybe four times my height. We're great swimmers, oh yes. And we can hold our breath underwater for a long time. I can almost swim halfway across underwater without coming up once for air."

Tommakee looked across the village. He guessed the outermost ring of lodges spanned probably a 200-yard diameter. The flooding itself was about double that distance. "That's pretty impressive Ono," he said.

"Thanks," Ono replied. "But you should see some of our strongest warriors. There's some who can almost swim the entire way across underwater."

Onomineese led them out of the forest proper and across a wide, flat plain that slowly sloped down to the water's edge. As they were walking, dozens of children much younger than Kaiyoo and Wayotel came running out to meet the new strangers. These little "pups" as Ono called them, stared and pointed, chattering among themselves. Many reached out and touched the hairy camel. Tommakee guessed they had never heard of such a creature like Yuba before, except maybe in old stories.

Then they encountered a line of warriors, standing still with firm, unreadable expressions. They were all stocky, heavily muscled, with thick black hair growing all over their skin and faces. Each warrior's waist was encircled with a belt holding up their brown breeches, and each one held a tall spear.

They don't wear moccasins, thought Kaiyoo, noticing everyone's bare feet. As they passed by the line of onlookers and started traversing the wooden bridge that connected the village to the shore, Kaiyoo thought he understood why.

On either side of the bridge, even though it was nearly night and the air temperature had cooled significantly, there were villagers swimming. Dozens of these Good People paddled and played in the water, climbing up onto the walkways and jumping back into the water. As Kaiyoo observed more of the village, it appeared that these Ahuizotl people were just as comfortable swimming from lodge to lodge as they would be walking around the walkways and across the bridges. *That's why they don't wear moccasins*, Kaiyoo thought. *They're constantly in and out of the water!*

Still more and more villagers met the newcomers on the bridge. It seemed everyone wanted a look at them. Ono walked proudly at their front, his head held high and smiling to everyone they passed.

The bridge opened out into a wide platform as it met the first of the village rings. Tommakee wondered at how solid and rigid the entire structure was. From the path above, it looked like the village may be floating on the water. Now he could tell the structure was firmly embedded in the river's bottom far below. There was no movement, no bounce in either the bridge or the wooden platform that comprised this ring of the village.

Their young guide stopped them in the middle of this open patio space. He stepped to the side, presenting the newcomers to the village elders, who were now standing right before them. Tommakee, still holding Yuba's reins, moved forward to stand next to the two boys in a line. The villagers continued crowding in, wanting a good look at the strangers. The children squirmed their way close to Yuba, still wanting to reach out and see if indeed the creature was real.

A squat, wrinkled elder spread his arms wide and smiled at them all. "Welcome, new friends. I am Tialoc, the chief of the Ahuizotl people." He extended one hand to the shoulders of each boy. "And a hearty welcome to you, young Nihuatl, and to you, young Tonal. You've stepped right out of the legends of old.

Our village is blessed to have you stay with us."

Surrounding the chief stood several grim-faced warriors, who appeared to be bodyguards or captains. After Tommakee introduced himself and the boys, a pair of older women stepped forward. They took turns speaking.

"We are sure you must be tired, hungry, and thirsty. We will show you to lodges where you can wash the traveler's dust from your feet and cleanse your hands for the evening meal."

The other woman continued, "Then we will escort you to the chief's lodge, where a special banquet is being prepared right this very minute. Please, follow us."

Tommakee bowed low. "We thank you for your kindness. But there is one matter I wish to speak to the chief about immediately. An urgent matter."

The chief waved the two older women to the side. He then stepped forward with his two war captains so that the four of them were close enough to all touch shoulders.

"I fear your village is in great danger, wise one," Tommakee whispered. "We were tracked here by Nagual warriors and..."

The chief nodded and placed one hand over Tommakee's heart. "I've been told of your bravery. The bravery of all three of you. And we already know of the Nagual. It is as the old story says, when the Age of the Sun nears its end, the Nagual and their master will again try to reclaim the world."

"I know two were severely hurt in the log slide…"

"They're dead," the chief said triumphantly. "Our scouts checked to be sure. We're safe for the current time."

Tommakee was insistent. "But there were more out there. I heard them. They were tracking us. They'll be back, and with a greater force next time."

Tialoc smiled. "Then we will deal with them when they arrive. It is not likely they will be back this evening. And we are heavily defended from attacks of all sorts."

Tommakee took a deep breath, obviously not believing the chief could be so inattentive to the danger they all were facing.

"I know you worry. You have a right to worry," Tialoc said slowly and quietly. "But I cannot allow my people to panic. We are a peaceful people. We live apart from the world. Few have ever left our village, and even fewer have ever visited us. But we do know how to fight to protect ourselves.

"If it will make you feel more safe, know this. Our warriors are on the highest alert, even if the rest of the villagers don't yet know the danger that is coming. Even now we are fortifying our defenses out of the eyesight of the rest of the village. Beginning tonight, we will be ready to remove the bridge to the shoreline. Then no one can harm us. We'll be completely safe.

"In the ancient days, when vast and powerful enemies approached us, they found our village impenetrable. Eventually, they decided we weren't worth the trouble and they left us alone. It happened before. It will happen again."

Knowing there was no use in pushing this any further, Tommakee just nodded. "I trust in your judgment, wise chief."

Tialoc smiled. "Your body and spirit need nourishment and rest. Go now with Wela and Chichitin. They will attend to you tired travelers. We will speak of the Nagual again later. In the company of our warriors and captains."

***

Tommakee and the boys followed the two old women. Onomineese never left their side as they walked. The crowd of children still trailed them. Occasionally, one would reach out and touch the camel's long shaggy hair.

Then they would all giggle and slap each other on the back and arms.

"Wise grandmothers," Ono said to the two old women as they softly padded down the decking between lodges, "These two young travelers would be very welcome in my family's lodge. If it's okay."

He looked to the two boys. "If you want. We have plenty of room since my older brother built his own lodge with his new wife earlier this summer. It was just after the Sun Festival that they pledged themselves. "

The two boys looked surprisingly at Ono. "You celebrate the Sun Festival here?" they both said, nearly in unison.

"Of course," Ono replied. "It's the biggest celebration of the year. Fires and food and swimming all day and all night in the warm water." Ono smiled and looked up at the first stars that were appearing in the deep violet sky. "It's the best night of the year."

Kaiyoo and Wayotel exchanged glances. The celebration at the Sun Festival in Atolaco had started out wonderful. But they both knew how that had ended in tragedy. Wayotel started to say something, but Kaiyoo touched his hand and shook his head. This wasn't the time or place to share such awful memories.

Chapter 5

The two boys slept soundly and comfortably, in a way they had not in over a month. As they pushed open the thick wooden door and emerged from Ono's family lodge the next morning, the sun was already an arm's length up into the sky, though it was mostly hidden behind quickly moving clouds.

Besides realizing they had slept late, both noticed the frigid air that prickled their bare chests. *Must be what hugging a porcupine would feel like*, Kaiyoo thought. Their breath blew out in white clouds, and they quickly slipped back inside the warmth of the lodge. Wayotel, wrinkling his nose, crawled back into his sleeping skins. Kaiyoo, on the other hand, was still intrigued by Ono's village. He quickly donned his layers of clothing and walked outside again.

It had been cold enough through the night to leave a skin of ice on the calm surface of the flooding, mostly where the water met the logs and rocks. Now, with the significant cloud cover, the ice wasn't in much danger of melting any time soon. It did disappear quickly, though, as it was broken off in handfuls by the "pups" and eaten. The youngsters laughed at each other as their long front teeth stung from crunching the ice chips.

Onomineese's family lodge was situated in the village's second ring from the center. It was not a huge building, but big enough to be comfortable. The boys had slept on soft, thickly padded cushions on the floor. There was no fire for light or heat inside, but the tightly interlocked wall timbers insulated the single room so they weren't cold. Fashioned to the interior walls were more thick furs and skins, most of which were stained in colorful, artistic patterns. A single door at one end of the lodge, also expertly crafted to prevent drafts, was only opened for someone to enter or exit.

Both Kaiyoo and Wayotel were mostly intrigued by a trap door in the floor at the end of the lodge opposite the door. Ono had proudly showed it to them when they had first arrived in the lodge. Smiling, Ono said, "All of our lodges have a tunnel down into the flooding below. For emergencies, my mother says, of course. But we like to use it whenever we can."

Ono encouraged the boys to try it out, but after touching the nippy water, Wayotel shivered and declined. Kaiyoo said, "Maybe we should wait until spring time," making Ono laugh.

***

When Kaiyoo exited the lodge, Ono's mother smiled at him and waved him over to her cooking fire. His eyes examined the fire bowl that extended out over the water, as did all of the fires in the village. Kaiyoo guessed that would help make sure no sparks ever caught the decks or bridges alight.

"That smells delightful, mother," Kaiyoo said remembering his manners. He smiled back and crouched down next to her.

"Try this." She handed him a warm, flat bread rolled up so that he could grasp it in one hand. After one bite, Kaiyoo's eyes widened. It was delicious! The bread was light and sweet, and inside it was filled with some sort of mashed red berries.

He chomped down several big bites. "Wonderful, thank you so much!" he exclaimed, once his mouth was finally empty.

As he ate, Kaiyoo watched her make more of these breakfast cakes. As each one was done cooking, she handed it to the boy.

"Your friend should awaken soon, or you may just end up eating his breakfast," Ono's mother chuckled.

"Where is Onomineese this morning?" asked Kaiyoo.

Ono's mother pointed across the village toward the side nearest the mountains. "He and his father are out training. They will return later."

***

Tommakee had been awake for some time, already spending quality time with the Ahuizotl traders at the open place that they used as a market. Tommakee really didn't have much to trade, nor did the Ahuizotl have much to offer. There were a few wooden tools, some furs, and a lot of different foods.

It appeared to Tommakee that the Ahuizotl didn't really buy and sell to each other. They simply exchanged wares or services, based on what each family lodge needed and each villager's own expertise.

Mostly, he was impressed by the great number of villagers who were constantly in the water. People were already swimming when he awoke at the break of dawn. The water temperature didn't seem to matter to them. They swam between the rings of the village just as much as they might walk around.

***

That night the central council lodge was packed full of elders and other prominent members of the village. They formed a semicircle around Kaiyoo, Wayotel, and Tommakee, who sat on soft blanket skins. A gentle, warm fire burned in the center of the lodge atop a wide, circular stone. The cinders floated gracefully up and out of the lodge through a hole at the top of the peaked ceiling. Chief Tialoc and his council of elders sat upon raised platforms, looking down at the three visitors and the gathered contingent of villagers and warriors crammed into the lodge to hear their tale.

The audience was silent. Tommakee had just finished sharing the tale of their travels, from leaving Kaiyoo's village, to the destruction of Atolaco, to their escape into the foothills of these very mountains. Kaiyoo and Wayotel added in the accounts they personally experienced, though most of the talking was left to Tommakee. The villagers were enraptured by the epic journey these three had so far survived.

After the story was completed, the only one moving about in the lodge was the village

Wa-Kama, an ancient and wrinkled woman that the three travelers could certainly relate to. The boys each had a Wa-Kama in their own village. Tommakee had never been to a village without one.

The Ahuizotl version was shorter, plumper, and walked hunched over. Her crooked staff seemed the only thing keeping her upright as she serenely shuffled around the fire to sit next to the visitors.

"Tell me about your dream, young one," the village Wa-Kama said slowly to Kaiyoo.

All eyes were on Kaiyoo as he hesitated briefly and then shared the entire vision he had had. He described the army hidden in the hillside, the transforming warriors, the ambush, and the black monster that had finally defeated the mighty Elk Guardian. Kaiyoo even somehow knew the name of the black beast that had appeared in his dream—*Concua Cahuayoh*.

Kaiyoo had told neither Wayotel nor Tommakee about his dream, and both were surprised by this new tale Kaiyoo shared with the council. Tommakee's mind stretched back to his life in the world before. The black beast, this *Concua Cahuayoh*, was known by a different name. It was called the Waheela, and it was one of the most formidable creatures ever described in the mythology of any civilization around the world.

It was described as being the Native American mythological equivalent of a dragon.

***

Wa-Kama was especially interested in this new enemy, and this was the only time she had interrupted the tale. Several times she posed a question of Kaiyoo and Wayotel, who were watching her ever so closely. Wayotel noticed that she had begun to slowly draw lines in the dust on the floor with the tip of her staff. Her eyes never left Kaiyoo's face, yet her hands, those ancient and delicate fingers, traced an intricate design on the ground before her.

Finally, Kaiyoo fell silent and he sat facing the Wa-Kama and the rest of the village elders. The only sound for quite some time was the light crackling of the fire as a little cloud of sparks would shoot upward and follow the smoke trail up out of the lodge.

Finally one of the elders spoke. A single word, a single name, "Moswa."

It was not a word or a name that either of the two boys recognized, but it seemed to carry some weight among the assembly. Grim faces slowly nodded, as glances were passed between the elders.

Kaiyoo stared deeply into Wa-Kama's eyes. She reminded him terribly of the Wa-Kama of his own village, and that brought back the memories of his family, his father. It all seemed so long ago, and yet everything had happened so quickly. Everything he knew, his whole life, had been whisked away. Tears started to well up in his eyes, and he fought to hold them back. He was a man now, not a crying child.

"So first Nahma and now Moswa," one elder exhaled softly, looking over to Chief Tialoc.

But the chief just slowly nodded. He knew the old prophecies, knew them well. They had been told and retold as myth and legend for a thousand years. If the great Guardians of the bear and elk had already been defeated, it didn't bode well for the lesser tribes.

Wayotel looked to Kaiyoo, whispering, "Who is Moswa?"

Tommakee leaned over and quietly answered, "He must have been the Elk Guardian, the one from Kaiyoo's dream."

Murmurs softly passed among the crowd.

The chief looked back and forth across the faces of his trusted council. "The *Concua Cahuayoh* comes from the darkness of the underworld. It will grow larger and become stronger and more powerful the longer it is in our world."

"Young one," the chief addressed Kaiyoo. "When was your vision? When did you see these events unfold?"

Kaiyoo thought for a moment before answering. "It was just after the night of the Sun Festival, honored father."

The council members exchanged glances before Wa-Kama spoke. "It's been in our world for at least a month. Likely more. It will soon be no longer bound to the earth as we are. It will be able to cover vast distances and to attack without warning."

The two boys looked at Tommakee for clarification. The old traveler sighed and stated grimly, "It will fly through the air."

Kaiyoo could barely comprehend this. The only creatures in their world that could fly were the insects, the birds. Even the largest birds he had ever seen had a wingspan the length of his outstretched arms. And their bodies were small comparatively. The creature in his dream was huge, heavy...greater in size than 10, maybe 15, grown men. How could this monster fly?

***

Wa-Kama could see that Kaiyoo and Wayotel, as well as most of the gathered audience, were highly distressed. "Young ones," she said loudly to the boys, though she was also addressing the entire room. "You know the story of Xoloctil and his brother?"

The great room fell silent. The two boys looked at each other and shook their heads. "No, honored mother," they said in near-unison. "Not truly."

Wa-Kama smiled. "It's a tale as old as time. In that age, long before the Good People walked the earth, in the time of the gods themselves, in a time before even the sun itself, a giant wolf was ravaging the land. It devoured most every creature it encountered. It destroyed the fields where it walked. It tore up mighty trees easily with its fangs.

"Xoloctil and his brother Mixtil, two of the Ancient Shepherds of the world, traveled far from their homes in the fiery, enlightened east to the icy wastes of the north, to the gates of the underworld where the great wolf had its lair. Mixtil wanted to slay the beast to protect the world. But Xoloctil actually wanted to kill it to take its powers. He wanted to rule the world himself.

"When they arrived at the gates of the underworld, the wolf stayed hidden in the darkness. Xoloctil and Mixtil, unafraid, charged in after it. After a fierce battle in which both brothers were wounded, they cornered the wolf, which was afraid of their torches. Mixtil distracted it with his torch while Xoloctil slit its throat.

"Mixtil was ready to leave, having accomplished the task of ridding the world of that monster. But even as he turned to head out of the underworld, Xoloctil was already skinning the wolf. In moments, he had removed the wolf's pelt and covered himself with it. The evil strength of the wolf began to creep into Xoloctil's body, giving him a dark power.

"The two brothers walked to the edge of the underworld, but suddenly Xoloctil could go no further. The great wolf pelt could not pass the borders of the underworld. 'Come with me, brother,' Mixtil implored. 'Leave that accursed pelt behind. It has led to only death and destruction in the world. Come back with me.'"

"But Xoloctil refused to leave. He snugged the pelt around his shoulders and slowly backed into the darkness."

"Mixtil called after him. 'I won't ever give up on you, brother. I'll leave out a light for you to follow when you tire of wearing that evil pelt. The light will be your way home. Dismayed at his brother's choice, Mixtil left the underworld. Once back on the earth, Mixtil looked for the best place to leave his guiding light for his brother to someday follow.

"He whistled loudly and an eagle flew to his outstretched arm. Mixtil handed over his torch, which the eagle took in its beak. Mixtil instructed the great bird to carry the torch every day from the far east, all the way up across the sky, and to put it out in the great sea beyond the western mountains. The eagle was told to do this each day.

"Every night the eagle flew back to relight the torch in the eastern land of fire. Then it made its journey again every day, lighting up the world. Mixtil's torch became the sun as we know it. And soon thereafter, more creatures flourished in the land. Then the Good People appeared."

"And Xoloctil?" asked Kaiyoo.

Wa-Kama gravely looked at the boys. "He searched and searched for a way out of his prison, for a prison the underworld had become to him. He had unlimited power but couldn't leave. He refused to leave. He hated the light his brother left in the sky for him. He wanted nothing better than to snuff it out.

"What Mixtil didn't realize was that the light was what prevented the great wolf's skin from leaving the underworld. And as long as Xoloctil wore it, drawing more and more of its evil power, he could never leave.

"Over time, as our Good People began to populate the earth, Xoloctil began to draw those with dark hearts to him. He also found darker, more foul beasts deep in the underworld that would do his bidding.

"Mixtil's torches would eventually burn down until there was nothing left. That was when that Age of the Sun would be over. And in that momentary time of darkness, as Mixtil fashioned a new torch to take the old one's place, devastation would occur in the world because Xoloctil could emerge from the underworld. His minions were always sent forth first, preparing for whatever cataclysm Xoloctil had planned."

"But in both of the previous Ages of the Sun, the Good People prevailed because of the great Guardians who rose up to defeat Xoloctil's dark armies. It was never easy, but the Guardians always succeeded."

Tialoc interrupted the story with a sigh. "This time, I fear, we are headed for a greater challenge. If Nahma and Moswa have been defeated, along with the other Nihuatl, who will the world rally around? Who will unite the remaining Guardians?"

Wa-Kama turned and smiled at the chief. "The legends of old described not a great and powerful Guardian who would lead the resistance. The legends spoke of a young one, aided by the power of the white from the four directions of the world. These four Good People with pale skin will help the young one gather the strength left in the world. The young one will unite the remaining Guardians to stand against Xoloctil."

Kaiyoo and Wayotel sat shocked at the feet of the village elders. How could it be that they were to be given such a monumental task?

"How can this be done?" Kaiyoo finally stammered. "I'm too young. I don't have the power to do this. I wouldn't know where to begin."

Pointing at Tommakee, Wa-Kama said, "There is already one pale-skinned man aligned to you, young one. Three more will be drawn to you. And as I look deeply into your face, into your aura, I see you already know your direction. You've had that told to you already."

"Nahma said my direction was the setting sun," Kaiyoo said softly.

"And as you follow the setting sun, young one, you will find your destiny."

***

"So what do we do?" asked another elder from the circle.

"We fight!" came a chorus from the younger warriors in attendance, breaking their silence. They nodded back and forth to each other, some flexing their muscles and slapping each other on the backs or shoulders.

One of the elders responded, "We cannot stand against the forces of the Nagual. They've grown strong. Stronger than the Nihuatl and the Mazatl. Our people are no match for them."

Again, more whispering passed among the gathered throng. The villagers hadn't started arguing yet, but Tommakee could see a definite difference in opinions was playing out.

"We do as we always have done," Chief Tialoc said calmly and forcibly. The room went silent, respecting the decision of the chief. "We stay hidden, here, far from the action of the world. The Ahuizotl people do not seek glory in battle. We have families, lodges here to protect. We are well hidden here. We are well protected here. But if enemies do find us, we also have strong defenses, as we have for thousands of years, through the ages of this world."

The chief turned to a decorated soldier on his left side. Tommakee assumed this must be the commander of the Ahuizotl warriors. The chief instructed him, "Peshawbe, I want you to double our guards both in and out of the village. Ensure our lookouts and scouts are well rested, and personally check that our defenses are fully prepared. If anything so much as a hare crosses into our borders, I want to know about it."

***

Most of the village had long since retired for the evening. But there were a few who were still awake in the depths of the darkness. Since the outsiders' arrival, the Ahuizotl warriors had been on steady guard, patrolling the forest, the flat land beyond the flooding, and the village walkways.

In the chief's lodge in the center of the village, the council fire slowly burned to embers. The Good People sitting around it had been silently waiting for an answer from their chief.

They had pieced together what little information they knew. Atolaco was ruined. None on the council had ever been there, but they all knew of its legendary size and importance as the center of civilization in the world. The Great Guardians of bear and elk were dead. The army of Xoloctal, both evil warriors and Nagual, were scattered all across the great plains, wiping out everyone who refused to join them. And perhaps even worse, if the boy's dream was any sort of revelation, the *Concua Cahuayoh* was loose upon the land. And it was hunting down the world's remaining warriors and Guardians.

Wa-Kama poked her crooked staff into the coals, carefully stirring them up. A small burst of light emanated from the fire, and the resulting warmth pleased the four men sitting next to her.

"Do you believe the child's tale?" one of the elders posed to Wa-Kama.

The old woman took a deep breath, then nodded her head. "This boy has greater power than we can understand. He speaks with the innocence of a child. He speaks of things he does not know, things he could not know. And yet, I have no doubt he has received training from Nahma himself. He saw the great Nihuatl's demise with his own eyes. And he saw the demise of Moswa with his inner eye."

Peshawbe, the decorated captain, nodded in agreement. "And do you believe these enemies will follow the travelers' here?"

Chief Tialoc exhaled slowly and loudly. "Whether enemies are tracking these three strangers to our valley is not the point. Enemies are moving through the world destroying everything in their path. We must consider that an attack on our village could be imminent."

The chief looked at each of his most trusted advisors seated with him. "Our defenses are solid, and they will provide warning and time to secure our people. We will have safety here in the middle of the flooding. But we need to prepare the village for winter. A winter perhaps like no others. A winter in which we might not be able to leave the flooding at all."

"Then we must have everyone begin preparations immediately," Wa-Kama said, and the men all nodded in agreement. "There's no time to lose."

***

Three more days passed. Kaiyoo and Wayotel easily melded into the daily routine of village life by joining Ono in all of his duties.

Kaiyoo was still disturbed by the meeting with the elders. He was disturbed by the pressure they were all placing upon him. Deep in his chest, his heart told him they were right, it was now his destiny to unite the Guardians in the world. It tied so tightly to the teachings of Nahma.

His thoughts and feelings, however, were overwhelming. It became so much easier to bury that destiny deep in his heart and focus his thoughts and feelings on being just a boy among friends in a friendly village.

Besides, there were so many things to do, so many things that quickly grabbed the attention of three boys.

The Ahuizotl people normally were busy this time of year, boosting their stores for the long winter ahead. But after Chief Tialoc's proclamation, everyone in the village worked extra by stockpiling provisions as a defensive measure. These people were still as good-natured and cheerful as they had been when the three travelers arrived. No one seemed unsettled by even the mere possibility of an attack, despite all of the extra preparations.

But few had free time to spend swimming for leisure. Even the youngest of children were engaged in collecting and hauling in green saplings from the loggers at the forest's edge. Baskets of foodstuffs were steadily streaming in from the forests. Fish and meats were drying in the smokehouses and giving off a wonderful aroma.

The village resembled a chaotic anthill more so than it did the legendary, peaceful city of Atlantis.

Only Tommakee remained visibly uneasy. His eyes were always turned to the surrounding forest, especially the main path that led down to the village. His attention was immediately drawn to any tree falling or disturbed flock of crows in the distance.

That evening, as the sun had already dipped behind the western mountains, Tommakee leaned against a railing. He was disturbed, but he showed it to no one, especially not the boys. He kept thinking back to the charge Wa-Kama had placed on Kaiyoo. It was a lot to expect of this mere boy. It was a lot to expect of anyone. He had given Kaiyoo's father his pledge that he would watch over the boy. The same for Wayotel.

And now they were on the verge of a mighty quest, one of mythic proportions. No matter how he pondered it, no matter how many different routes his mind took to even fathom it, Tommakee found this quest unattainable.

The longer they stayed in this village, the less likely it was that they would leave.

The longer they stayed in this village, the more likely they would encounter an attacking army.

So that's it, Tommakee thought to himself. *You've decided. You're really going through with this crazy plan. Guide the boys into the unknown. Try to save the world.*

Yes, I guess I've decided. And we'd better consider leaving soon. Before winter really hits. Before more Nagual track us here.

As if in answer to his thoughts, a horn blew in the distance, echoing in the trees to the east. Ono, Kaiyoo, and Wayotel quickly sprinted up to Tommakee, squeezing through the suddenly animated throng of villagers around them.

"That's the warning signal," Onomineese said, hurriedly.

Steamy breath rising into the twilight's chill, warriors continued to race up into the hills, disappearing into the thick forest. All carried thick, two-handed spears that were nearly as tall as themselves. Most wore a type of armor consisting of hundreds of overlapping wooden disks stitched tightly to heavily padded overcoats.

Women and children ran to their lodges, crouching in doorways waiting to see what would happen.

"What's going on?" Wayotel asked, panic starting to emerge in his voice.

"Something's approaching the village."

Not all of the village's warriors headed for the forest. Several dozen men remained behind on the bridge to the shoreline. They immediately leapt over the railing and into the frigid water. As a defense mechanism, the bridge supports were counterbalanced by huge stones. In this way, the bridge could be raised or lowered. Once the men removed the supports, the bridge slowly sank beneath the surface in less than a minute. Only once the long wooden structure was completely submerged and not even visible from above did the divers resurface, swimming back to the outermost ring of the village.

Interval

The Light
(part 1)

Rain continued to drizzle outside the coffee shop's lone window. Outside, the tiny town's silence was only broken by the roar of the occasional semi-truck speeding by on the highway. Later in the afternoon or evening, the rain would undoubtedly turn to snow. But for now, the late morning sun, hidden behind dense cloud cover, kept the precipitation in liquid form rather than frozen.

Inside the little shop, a trio of fluorescent light fixtures kept the room aglow in whitewashed light. Every few minutes, a bar in the room's central light fixture gave a little buzz and flickered.

Only two of the shop's eight red-checkered tables were occupied. By the window, an old man poked at his biscuits, apparently absorbed by the growing puddles in the gravel parking lot. He didn't seem to notice the gravy running down his long gray beard.

Large mounds of dirty snow were ever so slowly melting in the upper 30-degree temperatures. Maple syrup collectors were undoubtedly loving the current forecast. Nights still remained below freezing, while the days warmed up just enough to keep the sap running.

At a table farthest from the door, a man and a woman sat across from each other. There was nothing conspicuous about either of them, just two small town folks having coffee and thumbing through a stack of papers. They could have been digging through pages of local antique dealers or possibly sealing a real-estate deal. Such meetings occurred often in little town coffee shops.

The woman, tall and lanky, kept her navy woolen overcoat tightly wrapped around her. She still wore her red knit hat, even indoors. The thin walls of the old coffee shop building didn't do much for keeping the March cold outside. The man across from her wore a red flannel jacket over top of a gray hooded sweatshirt.

"It's so hard to believe almost five years have passed so quickly," Agent Brock said, sipping his coffee. "The agency's gone. Headquarters is gone. All of the agents are gone."

"Or gone into hiding," Agent Grace added.

Agent Brock gave a half-hearted smile. "Like us."

Their meeting was no mere coincidence.

He continued to browse through the papers, separating some out into different stacks on the table's small surface. They were computer printouts.

"I can't tell you how much I appreciate this, Agent Grace," he said.

Both of her hands on her mug, she replied, "My pleasure. Agent Bradley wanted you to have these. He knows what you're up against."

"What we're all up against," Agent Brock said, his eyes still locked on the papers. "I'm sorry he's gone. Agent Travis always spoke highly of him."

"He was a good partner, a good mentor," Grace sighed, looking into her coffee. "And a good friend."

Brock thought about his own mentor, Agent Travis, who'd disappeared in the rubble of the disaster at headquarters. They had been partners for a few months. Agent Travis had been training him to become a full-fledged field agent. Now he was gone from this world.

Across the street, a huge, hand-painted billboard stood next to a building half its size, loudly proclaiming, "Big Bill's Bait Shop: Beer, Bullets, & Booze." Across the bottom corner was tacked on another plywood cutout that read, "Pasties, Smoked Fish, Coin Laundry."

As he neared the bottom of the stack, those papers with the most recent dates, he paused. His hands instinctively slid up his neck to the back of his head, fingers pushing through his beard—which wasn't allowed back when he was officially on the job—and long hair— now sprinkled with gray hairs, even though his 30th birthday wasn't for another five months. His fingers laced together behind his head, and he closed his eyes, remembering back to that fateful day, five years earlier.

***

Agent Brock was slowly chewing a piece of beef jerky when his phone beeped. He tapped the accept button on his touchscreen and put the phone to his ear, his left elbow leaning absentmindedly out the window of his non-descript, government-issue sedan.

"Brock here," he answered, licking a bit of gristle from his top teeth.

"This is an emergency, code 13," the voice on the other end said. "You're being recalled to headquarters, effectively immediately."

"What's going on?" Brock asked, sitting a bit more upright.

"We'll brief you when you arrive."

Agent Brock exhaled slowly, trying to calculate the trip time in his head. Driving from the village of Watersmeet in the far western end of Michigan's Upper Peninsula to the state capital of Lansing would take him six and a half to seven hours, depending on the traffic and the crossing of the Mackinac Bridge.

He looked at his watch, and then spoke into his phone. "I can be there around 6 or so…" he began.

"We don't have time for delays, agent," the voice cut him off. "We're bringing you in."

Confused, Agent Brock said, "I don't quite understand."

The voice responded through his phone. "You'll meet your transport at the Riverside Café in Iron River. I suggest you get moving, now."

The phone went dead, and Agent Brock exhaled slowly, staring straight out the windshield of his sedan at the fields and woods beyond.

***

As Agent Brock pulled into the parking lot of the Riverside Café, he saw the usual line of beaten-up pickups and station wagons he had grown accustomed to in the few days he had been traversing the western Upper Peninsula. His eyes scanned each vehicle carefully, unable to believe any one of them was his contact here.

As he rounded the far side of the building, Agent Brock gave a chuckle. His transport was waiting for him.

Standing next to the passenger door of a dusty ambulance was another agent, easily recognizable by his navy blazer, dark slacks, and white button-up shirt with black tie. The dark gray clouds reflected off his aviator sunglasses, worn even though there was no sunshine for miles.

Why would they send me an ambulance? Brock pondered. *I could drive just as fast in my own sedan.*

The driver stiffly strode over and shook hands. "I'm Agent Thomas. And you're late."

"Nice to meet you, too," Brock answered sarcastically.

"Lock it," Agent Thomas said icily, nodding at the sedan. "I'll take your keys."

Brock grabbed his travel bag from the back seat, clicked the car remote, and handed over the keys. Then the two men climbed into the ambulance's front seats in silence.

***

Agent Brock understood their mode of transport quickly. U.S. 2 wasn't normally a busy highway anyway, but every vehicle pulled aside as the ambulance shot up the hill out of town. It made for unimpeded travel.

It was silent in the cab. Agent Thomas was in full concentration, both hands gripping the steering wheel like a NASCAR driver. Within moments, the ambulance was cruising at 80 miles per hour.

Even Brock was uncomfortable with their speed in such a large-profile vehicle, though he would never say so. The ambulance rattled and jostled, and more than once Brock felt his stomach lurch as it seemed the vehicle's tires left the pavement.

The varying shades of green blurred together at the sides of the highway. What otherwise would have been a fine day to travel across the wilderness of the U.P. became lost as the line between urgency and recklessness narrowly edged together.

Still, Agent Thomas stared straight ahead. He said not a word, nor did he look away from the road.

Not even five miles out of town, Brock's eyes suddenly widened in surprise and fear. He could see a line of cars stopped on the highway, the swirling lights of a pair of state police cruisers blocking the road only a half-mile ahead. Agent Brock swore, and he fumbled with clicking his seat belt in anticipation of the upcoming brakes.

His hands slipped. He just couldn't get it buckled.

Luckily, it didn't matter. The ambulance shot right by the line of cars without slowing. The shiny blue state police car blocking the westbound lane backed up just in time to avoid a collision. If the officer had the briefest moment of confusion at seeing a man in a suit and tie driving the ambulance rather than the normal outfit of a paramedic behind the wheel, he didn't have time to give a second glance. Once the state cruiser slipped back to block the road, the ambulance and its unusual driver had already passed beyond sight around a wooded curve.

***

Just 28 seconds. That's how long it took between passing the police barricade and finally coming to a stop. Agent Brock knew it exactly because he had counted each tick of the second-hand as it marched around his military watch. He had given up trying to buckle the seatbelt and had his hands firmly planted on the dashboard in a futile attempt at survival, should they have crashed. It was probably just as well that he had locked his elbows out, because Agent Thomas did bring the ambulance to a fairly rapid stop just out of sight from all of the vehicles behind them.

Slowly, Brock turned his head to face the driver, his fingers still digging deeply into the vinyl dashboard, his lungs spastically trying to refill themselves. It was at that moment that Brock realized he had been screaming.

Agent Thomas swiveled and gave his passenger a wide, toothy grin. His eyes were still lost behind the shiny aviator glasses. "This is your stop. Have a nice day."

Brock's anger at Agent Thomas dissipated instantly when he saw the plane.

Yes, there was a small Cessna jet sitting right in the middle of U.S. 2. Two men, apparently the pilots, were standing right next to its folding air stair.

***

"You mean you've actually landed a plane, right here on the highway?" Brock asked as he stared dumbfounded at the jet waiting on the asphalt. It was parked sideways on the highway, nose to tail measuring from one shoulder of the road to the other. A thick screen of cedar trees formed the backdrop to this completely unexpected scene.

"It's not our normal method for picking up passengers, but it's not out of the range of possibilities either," replied the captain with a smug grin.

Brock looked at where the highway eventually made another curve far ahead in the distance. "It may be silly of me to ask, but do we have enough room for takeoff?"

"Plenty of room," the pilot nodded. "We only need three-quarters of a mile. You'd never believe some of the places we've taken off from or landed in. Now, stories aside, Agent Brock, if you will be so kind as to buckle in, we are in a bit of a hurry."

Hurry was the understatement of the day. The agent climbed the couple of steps into the jet's cabin, followed by the pilots. It was nothing special inside — more or less a flying taxi — not at all what Brock had imagined a private jet to be. There was no wet bar, no flight attendants. Just two single rows of seats.

The co-pilot nudged a small Coleman cooler toward Brock with his foot. "Here's your in-flight service, agent."

Brock lifted the lid to see a 6-pack of A&W Root Beer and a jar of Planters cashews. He set the cooler on the seat next to him.

Just before the co-pilot slipped into his seat, he mentioned, "Oh, and no communications until we're airborne, please.

Those warnings the airlines give — yes, cell phones *can* interfere with navigational equipment, especially with small jets. We don't want to end up floating in Green Bay."

Brock nodded. There really wasn't anyone he could call anyway. He had been trying to text and call Agent Travis for several days now, but there had been no response. *Probably off in his own world, his own problems to deal with*, thought Brock.

The jet spun effortlessly on the highway. Brock did notice they had chosen a long, flat stretch of U.S. 2 that had been widened with passing lanes on both sides. Within seconds, the Cessna taxied down the highway and zipped into the air.

***

The flight was over quickly, and an agency car met them at the Lansing Capital Region Airport. Agent Brock was shuttled quickly into the back seat of a typical Agency sedan, which headed into downtown Lansing rather than toward the university campus. A pair of agents he didn't know sat up front. Neither spoke during the entire trip.

"We're not going to headquarters?" Brock asked, puzzled, as the car finally slipped into a parking structure. He could tell they were only a few blocks from the Capitol Building because he had seen its dome just over the tops of the nearby buildings. Agent Brock was originally from the metro Detroit area, and he had completed his criminal justice degree at Penn State before joining the NSA. He wasn't completely familiar with Lansing, but he did know the Capitol Building was about four miles away from the Agency headquarters at the eastern end of campus.

A curt, deep voice answered from the front seat, "The director will brief you on everything when you meet."

A brisk walk and elevator ride later, Agent Brock found himself in a huge hotel conference room. Temporary walls had been made from banks of equipment and computers as well as cubical dividers. The two agents, still wearing their trademark sunglasses, escorted him through the maze of too many people crammed into too small a space. His mind was on overload trying to take in so many details around him. He was pretty sure there were a lot of familiar faces — he didn't know any of them well — but certainly there were people he had seen from the headquarters building.

"What is this place?" he asked the agents just ahead of him.

One of them looked over his shoulder. "Temporary headquarters."

***

Director Mason folded his hands on the table in front of him. *Funny how agitation and nervousness can look the same*, thought Agent Brock. The young agent knew, however, that his boss was holding back, not giving him the entire story.

The two of them were seated in a small, unadorned room at the back of the busy main conference room, serving as the new headquarters. Brock accurately guessed the upper brass of the agency would have more secure temporary offices than the rank and file out in the open space.

"At approximately 1300 hours last Saturday afternoon, our main headquarters building was attacked," the director began. "From the initial reports of the survivors, it seems we were sabotaged from within."

"I don't mean to be insensitive, but may I ask why I'm back?"

Director Mason continued as if Brock hadn't spoken. "Most of the building was destroyed. The terrorists used quite an arsenal—small arms, explosives, incendiaries—honestly, agent, the entire building has been gutted by fire."

"And the survivors?"

"Treated, debriefed. There was one, however, who somehow managed to make it out of the deepest hellhole. He's been moved into the burn unit at Sparrow Hospital in Lansing. Obviously he's in critical condition, in and out of consciousness." The director grunted, shaking his head slightly. "Craziest thing though. When he did wake, despite the pain, he asked for you."

Agent Brock was even more puzzled. He was new enough to the Agency that he really didn't know anyone who worked at headquarters, except for the director. He fumbled for a response. "I, uh, sir, don't really know…"

"I believe you remember Professor Charles," the director interrupted.

"He's the lone survivor?"

"It appears that he and his team were the targets."

"What about Agent Travis?"

The Director took a deep breath and eased it out slowly. "I'm sorry, but it doesn't appear he made it."

All of the wind sailed out of Agent Brock's chest, and he slumped back in his chair.

***

"I don't know how much you know about our special projects division," Director Mason probed, studying the younger man's face carefully. "How much did Agent Travis or the professor share with you before you were sent back into the field?"

Brock shrugged his shoulders. His mind was still racing with everything he had been told in the past few minutes. Even though he tried to answer the question, Brock's focus kept circling back to the loss of his mentor. "It was mentioned...once or twice...I really don't know anything about it. Director, I just can't believe he's gone. Do we know what...how?"

"Agent Brock, I'm going to be upfront with you. We lost a huge chunk of the Agency's manpower yesterday afternoon. We're talking everybody from the think tank to the muscle. From what we can tell, there were over 300 casualties, and two-thirds of the bodies haven't even been located yet. The bottom floors, our special projects labs, appear to be completely buried in the cave-in. Structurally, the building appears fairly well undamaged from the outside since it's still standing. But inside, the floors all gave way and collapsed. Inside, it's like a canyon, dropping a hundred feet down to the rubble below.

"I still don't know how the professor got out of there — there's no logical explanation for it. But he did make it out. Now, he's fighting for his life, and the prognosis doesn't look good. He seems to have the only clues as to what happened."

"Hasn't anyone been there to question him when he's coherent?"

"We have security with the professor round-the-clock. A number of our people have tried speaking to him, but he just won't talk to any of us. He just keeps asking for you, and then he turns away and passes out again."

***

The debriefing with the director was filled with all sorts of awkward silences and long stares. Brock had the feeling he was being set up. Somewhere, somehow, someone had connected him to this tragedy. The professor was a big wig at the Agency, and he was asking for this nobody of a young agent. The Professor couldn't (or wouldn't?) talk to anyone else.

Director Mason found this far too suspicious for his liking. The kid knew something. Or the kid was connected to something. Maybe the spy in the Agency was tied to Professor Charles and this kid. Nothing was out of the realm of possibilities. General Nichols and the Department of Defense would be arriving the next day, and they wanted answers. They wanted someone to hang for this. And if they couldn't find someone responsible, they would take a scapegoat instead.

In the end, Agent Brock was sent, again with escort, to the hospital to meet with the professor.

***

Brock's current escort stopped at the elevator as he walked the last hundred feet himself down the brightly lit, sterile hospital hallway. A new pair of agents, both goliaths, guarded a room in the intensive care unit. One stood next to the closed door. The other agent was squeezed into a chair that was designed for someone half his size. Both wore the customary sunglasses.

Brock showed his identification, and the hulking guard tapped on the door. "Agent Taylor?" the guard asked in a deep voice. "He's here."

Whoa, Brock thought as the door opened and a beautiful, petite woman stepped into the hallway. Her long, deep red hair was a blast of color against her white lab coat and the dark suits of the two hulking agents. *I didn't know they made agents that weren't behemoths.*

His eyes must have given away his thoughts because the redhead suddenly assailed him.

She stepped right up to Brock, pointing into his face and staring at him through semi-squinted eyes. "I'll give you two minutes with the professor, max. In his condition, he can't take any sort of shock to his system — it would kill him, you know. No shop talk, nothing to get him excited. I'm watching you."

Agent Brock walked cautiously through the door and over to the hospital bed. The fiery Agent Taylor was right on his heels. A nurse had just finished checking the readouts on several machines and was on her way out the door.

Brock looked down at the old, tired man who lay wrapped in bandages from head to foot. Only a few patches of skin were even visible, though Professor Charles's face and right hand were seemingly untouched by any burns. Brock remembered the old man's wild, wispy hair from their car ride only a week before.

Wow! Had it all happened that quickly? Was it really only a week ago that he and Agent Travis had chauffeured the old man to the Agency headquarters? And now that building, the entire organization, was nearly wiped clean from the face of the earth.

The patient gave a slight gasp and then croaked as he whispered, "Agent, would you be so kind as to get an old man a cup of water? I'm ever so thirsty."

Agent Taylor reached over to grab a thin, plastic Solo cup from the nearby counter, but was stopped by the old man.

"Not the nasty stuff from the tap," he whispered again. "They must have...some decent bottled water...somewhere in the building."

"Of course, sir. I'll be right back." She shot Agent Brock another narrow-eyed glare, perhaps an even more forceful way of saying "don't let him die while I'm gone" than if she had spoken a word at all.

Professor Charles gently took Brock's hand and smiled wearily until the door closed with a click. Then the young agent was taken by surprise as the old professor's demeanor changed. The gentle fingers now clutched Brock's, pulling him down closer to the old man's face. Professor Charles's eyes darted cunningly around the room, ensuring they were alone. Then he spoke with clarity. "We don't have much time until she gets back. I brought you here for a reason. I need your help, Travis needs your help."

"I'm sorry, sir, but Agent Travis is dead," Brock sputtered, trying to hold back tears.

"No, he's not," the professor sputtered right back. Even though the old man had been tricking the agents this whole time, his injuries were real. It was still a struggle to speak. "He went through the machine. The time machine. With the other two. They all escaped. And no one knows it but you and me."

The old man coughed for a couple of seconds, getting his wind back. "They'll need help getting back. You must find that portal."

"But how? Where?"

The old man forced a folded note into Agent Brock's hand. It was tiny and wrinkled as the professor had concealed it for many hours. "Start there. You'll find all of my notes, everything Travis and I had done. And don't trust anyone."

"Not even our own Agents?"

"Especially not them." Professor Charles now had a wild look in his eyes. "There's a spy in the Agency." He paused, getting his breath back. "No idea who it might be."

He went into a coughing fit again. When it cleared, he continued. "But beyond that, the Defense Department will be taking over now. They'll rein everyone in until they get to the bottom of this. It could take months, years, time we don't have. They're already pulling the plug on all of our projects, I'm sure of it. Agent Travis needs your help. The world needs your help."

The young man slipped his hand free from Professor Charles's grip and straightened up, staring blankly at the far wall of the room. His thoughts were again swirling, putting all of these pieces together. The problem was that too much of the puzzle was missing. And the professor was right—the military was already taking charge. Brock thought back to his conversation with the director. His mind then raced back to the agent who died having returned through the portal...

If Agent Travis was still alive—but the military wouldn't do anything to help him—

"You trusted Agent Travis, and now you need to trust me," the professor gave Brock his slightly crooked, grandfatherly smile.

Pursing his lips, Agent Brock gave the professor a slight nod. "What should I do?"

"First, you need to get out of here. Fast. They'll try to lock you in first, since you're already down here. Follow the clues I've set for you. The fate of the world is in your hands now."

Suddenly, the professor's eyes rolled back up beneath his eyelids, and his battered and bandaged body began to shake spasmodically. The hospital bed bounced and grated against the floor. Several machines began beeping and wailing loudly, only adding to the chaos.

Agent Brock looked up as the hospital room door slammed open and Agent Taylor burst in. She threw the bottle of water at the trashcan and shot an accusatory glare at Brock.

"I didn't do anything," Brock stammered, suddenly feeling very much out of place. "The seizures just started. Can I do something?"

As abruptly as they started, the seizures stopped. The old man lay lifeless on the hospital bed.

"Get out of here," the agent growled, her eyes shooting daggers at him. "You've done enough already."

As the agent stepped around the bed to hit the nurse's call button, Professor Charles opened one eye and gave Brock a wink before returning to his pretense of sleep.

Needing no further prodding, Agent Brock slipped out of the door and immediately plotted his escape from the hospital. As soon as he stepped outside, he was met by the pair of security agents.

"She needs you both, right now!" Brock jabbed his thumb at the door. The ruse worked, and he was pushed aside as the two behemoths fought each other to squeeze through the doorway first. Seeing his momentary window of opportunity, Agent Brock darted down the hallway toward the emergency stairwell away from the elevators.

***

Brock was brought back to the present by Agent Grace, speaking to him from across the table. "Refill?" The shop's one waitress had left the pot.

"Huh? Oh, yes, please," he answered.

"What are you thinking about?" she asked.

Agent Brock took a deep breath and exhaled slowly. "I'm certain this has to do with the Paulding Light."

"Well, mystery lights have always been associated with natural portals all over the world," Agent Grace said. "In Europe they were known as the Will O' Wisps. In west Texas, there are the Marfa Lights. The Gurdon Light in Arkansas. Brown Mountain Lights in western North Carolina. The Hornet Spooklight on the border between Missouri and Oklahoma. The Ghost Light in Saskatchewan, Canada."

"My last assignment with the agency was to find the portal here."

"Yes, the one Agent Mitchell supposedly reappeared through."

"It's got to be tied with the Paulding Light. It's just too coincidental. You know, I was just starting my investigation when everything fell apart at headquarters."

He carefully shared with her the details of being quickly whisked out of the U.P. and visiting the ruined building almost five years ago. He didn't quite mention the quest he had been on during the last five years, though. He didn't quite know for sure that he trusted her fully. Not yet. There may be time in the future to share those stories, but it wasn't this morning.

"Well, it's a good thing Agent Bradley had the foresight to print all of his and Travis's notes," Brock said. "Otherwise, everything would have disappeared."

"It did disappear," Agent Grace replied. "Agent Bradley heard what happened at headquarters and the first thing he did was to get a backup of it all. That was just minutes before the agency pulled the plug on the network. What you're looking at here I found stored on a key drive that he had squirreled away in a storage locker at the Milwaukee County Zoo. No one knows we have this information. Not the agency, not the *Brethren*, no one."

Agent Brock stared into his coffee. "*Brethren*," he whispered. Their old nemesis.

Agent Grace said what was on both of their minds. "Generally, they keep a low profile, stepping in occasionally, trying to thwart our progress. But now that the end of the world's Fifth Age is quickly approaching, they're siding with the ancient darkness that wants to regain power."

"The *Brethren* has been around for hundreds, maybe even thousands of years," Brock sighed. "They haven't done anything significant in recorded history. Then they made their boldest move ever by attacking the agency headquarters back in 2011. They assumed the End of Days was 2012, as did everyone at that time."

"You've read the notes," Grace interrupted. "You know what happened that changed all of our thinking. The newly found Mayan inscriptions that changed everything." She chuckled. "I'd have loved to see their faces when the end of the world didn't happen."

"Yes, but they didn't have access to that new information."

"I'll bet they have it now," Grace countered.

"2017?" Brock said, more a statement than a question.

"Yes, 2017," the woman answered. "A Dogman year, as you well know."

Brock sipped his coffee. "Not just a coincidence, is it?"

"Nothing at this point is coincidental." Grace said. "The pieces are moving on this chess set. They're moving more quickly all the time."

"And far too often their moves are hidden," Brock added.

***

"So what do you think will happen next?" she posed.

Agent Brock rubbed his beard thoughtfully. "The Dogman will appear, I'm certain of it. According to these notes, it will all start at the tip of the Lower Peninsula. That's where it left off."

He thought deeply for a moment before continuing. "Something Agent Travis once told me. A gut feeling of his. It wasn't something he'd written down. I didn't see it in any of these papers, which is a good thing, I think. That means the *Brethren* probably don't know it yet. Agent Travis believed the

Dogman was searching for something around Twin Lakes."

"And you don't think the Dogman found it yet, whatever it is?"

"I think Agent Travis was pretty sure. The creature was spotted in the Twin Lakes area for almost an entire year, right through to the end of December 2007. It spent the entire year searching for something. Otherwise, it would have continued moving north as it had done for decades."

Agent Grace stared at her companion. "What would it be searching for?"

"I think I know. Let me walk you through my theory. Besides being based on Agent Travis's notes, there's that diary."

"What diary?" asked Agent Grace.

"The one that TV-reality show had. Okay, let's start with the diary first. The TV show mentioned that the diary belonged to a French explorer from Fort Mackinac. A fur trader. The diary mentions the explorer having taken an artifact from a burial mound far to the south. His companions were killed mysteriously. The artifact was a necklace of claw-shaped totems. Gemstones. The explorer wrote that he had to trade these 'claws' for food from the various tribes he encountered as he walked his way back north to Fort Mackinac. They must have been some sort of precious stones because he was able to secure himself a peaceful retirement once he arrived back at the fort, where he lived out the remainder of his days.

"I've been studying the history of the straits area very carefully over these past five years. Did you know that the Sauk and Ojibwe sacked Fort Mackinac in 1763? It was just after the Pontiac Rebellion at Fort Detroit. There is no mention of that fur trader's name in the rolls at the fort, nor any record of his death. It was unlikely he lived long enough anyway to see the deadly lacrosse game that led to the death of all the British soldiers.

"But if he had, then perhaps he was killed and heaped in with the burned bodies. It was said the French were spared, but that too is only according to legend. Regardless of how or when he died, we have no idea what happened to the man's effects, post mortem."

Grace interrupted him. "But, if the diary had managed to survive centuries of abuse, including the massacre at the fort, certainly those jewel-claws must have survived too."

Brock took a sip of his coffee. "So here's what I'm thinking. The Dogman has been following the trail of those jewel-claws, which was like a the trail of breadcrumbs left by the fur trader as he traveled north."

"What would the creature be collecting the gems for?" asked Agent Grace.

Brock shrugged his shoulders. "I have no idea. It's kind of a longshot theory, but it sorta makes sense to me. I think the Dogman is collecting these. And I think there may still be one or more left in the tip of the Lower Peninsula, perhaps even still buried in the fort itself."

Grace leaned in closer across the table. "Now, let's say the Dogman is able to find all of these gems. Then what does it do?"

Looking her dead in the eyes, Brock whispered, "Agent Travis thinks it's coming here. To find the portal."

"It'll have to cross the straits first. You're thinking the Mackinac Bridge?"

Brock nodded. "That's my best guess. I know the creature can swim, but I don't see it swimming five miles in near-freezing water, especially if it tries to cross early in the year."

"It could cross if the straits were frozen," Agent Grace posed.

"Always a possibility in January or February, I know. But I don't think it's ready to cross. Not yet."

"Why's that?" Grace asked.

"I don't think it's found everything it needs—all the gemstones. I think it needs to complete its collection. I believe it'll start its search again in about nine months, just after the start of the new year. 2017. And we'll start hearing about it in the news.

"Once it has the full collection, then it'll cross the straits. Then it'll be headed here."

Leaning back, stunned against her chair, Agent Grace asked, "Why would the Dogman be headed all the way across the U.P.?"

"It's got something to do with this End of Days prophecy. 2017. The recalculation of the Mayan long-count calendar. Agent

Travis thinks the Dogman's going to let something cross into our world. Something evil. Something powerful enough to destroy our world."

"Maybe that's what it needs the gemstones for," Agent Grace hypothesized. "To somehow open the portal."

Brock nodded in agreement. "That does sound like a reasonable guess. And the portal that something's going to come through isn't too far from we're sitting right now. We need to find it before the Dogman does. Plus, I'm on the lookout for anything, or anyone, who might come through that portal."

"What do you mean, anyone? Tell me what you know."

Agent Brock hesitated, then finally decided to share with her about what Professor Charles had told him in the hospital. Agent Travis and the other two had crossed over using the time portal machine. He didn't know for sure, but the other two were likely the two doctors, the experts that Professor Charles had brought in to help.

This was information that no one else, in five years' time, had known. It had been assumed by everyone in the organization, everyone in the government, that these three men had been pulverized and were still buried deep in the rubble of the headquarters building.

***

"You think the *Brethren* will have access to all this?" Travis asked, putting the various piles of papers into one stack.

Grace nodded. "It's my understanding they had a mole in our agency for some time now. That's what led to the catastrophe. I'd assume they have all of the information we have."

"Maybe we have a slight advantage then," Brock said. "We have just a little bit of intel that one else on the planet has."

"We're outlaws, you know," Agent Grace said softly. "Running from the *Brethren*, running from the National Security Agency. There's no one we can trust. No one we can turn to for help."

"Just each other," Brock said with a small hint of a smile. He dropped a couple of dollars on the table next to the empty coffee mugs.

"So now what do we do?" she asked.

"We lay low," Agent Brock answered. "We disappear again. Are you heading back to Wisconsin?"

"My aunt's old farmhouse. It's been a good refuge so far. And I can still keep tabs on everything that's going on through my connection inside the D-O-D."

Agent Grace stood up. "What about you? You're still driving for that vending company?"

Brock jingled his key ring. "Filling vending machines with cigarettes and snacks might not seem glorious, but it pays the bills. It keeps me mobile and pays in cash. I'm pretty much off any sort of government radar. And I'm on my own schedule. I've got the freedom to spend time poking around. I'll find that portal yet, mark my words."

Book 4
Arrival

Chapter 1

Dim, diffused light started to increase in intensity as the blackness faded. It was like awakening from a deep sleep, when your eyes have yet to blink away the last remnants of the dream world.

The fingers of Agent Travis's hands reached out in front of him ever so slowly. But they were hard to control, hard to move with any sort of real control. It was as if he was underwater, pushing against the hydraulic forces all around him.

He realized that was exactly where he was.

A quick blink of the eyes brought him to his senses. Instinctively, his mouth opened and it was immediately filled with water. He panicked, spastically thrashing his arms up toward the light above as if they could somehow pull him up out of this cold wetness.

And then he was out! Travis's head,

shoulders, and arms exploded up through the water's surface. A moment of dread rocked him as he tried to breathe in air and only sucked in water. His feet kicked and pushed down on something hard as he coughed and sputtered, spewing out the water he had swallowed.

The agent's body lurched forward, his feet still propelling him, and he fell to his hands and knees as the rocky bottom sloped up toward the bank. Water sprayed from his lips and nose, trickling down his face in little streams. Cold air was sucked into his greedy lungs.

Eyes blinking away the moisture, Travis was just starting to turn his head around and look for his companions when something seized his left shoulder in a stone-like grip. It was like being caught in a gigantic pair of pliers. Pain instantly drove right through his skin to the bone. The agent's mind was shrieking, but only a coughing gasp came out along with more water and phlegm.

Stars danced before his eyes as his body was roughly yanked upward into the air and spun around.

A moment later, Travis's feet dangled a foot above the ground and he was face to face with a brutish, humanoid colossus. The creature stared at the man with beady, black eyes, all too small for its huge, misshapen head. The behemoth's bulbous nose was nearly the size and shape of a plump pear, a fitting description since its skin was also an earthy and pale greenish-brown. If ever he had had a chance to believe in ogres of legend, he was seeing one in the flesh right now.

The agent nearly gagged from the putrid stench of the creature's breath, continuously blasting him in the face. And his shoulder stung from the tight grip of its massive hand. To make matters worse, the creature tightened its grip, showcasing its powerful strength in holding Travis up by only one of its huge arms.

A sharp command from behind the behemoth caused it to turn away. A high-pitched voice was barking orders in a language Travis didn't recognize. Whatever it was, the words were enough to make the brute suddenly release its grip. The agent fell to the ground, smashing his hip and elbow against a hard chunk of stone.

This day didn't start out particularly well an entire world away, and it wasn't getting any better here, wherever they were.

***

As the shrill, authoritative voice droned on, seeming to chastise the giant, Travis finally gathered his wits enough to scan his surroundings and take stock of his situation.

He still wore his white collared shirt, which was now rather mangled and beginning to stain with the blood that trickled down from a number of cuts and deep scrapes on his shoulder. His jacket and tie—and probably his handgun—had somehow disappeared. He was covered with a colorless mud that surrounded the deep pond from whence, he believed, he had arrived in this world.

Gray, lifeless clouds hung low over the land. In all, it was quite a dreary place.

The giant beast towered above him. It was at least eight feet tall, thick as an oak, from wide, flat and bare feet to the curved, ram-like horns atop its head.

Hard, pebbly skin stretched over bulging muscles. It wore only a ragged loincloth that hung to its knobby knees. The rest of its body was exposed to the cool air.

That thought made the agent shiver a bit. Only now did he notice the temperature, especially as the moisture evaporated quickly from his clothing, chilling his skin.

Yes, they were in a different world. A cold world.

They. They! Travis couldn't believe he didn't register it sooner. His two companions were only 30 feet away. Both Michael Camaron and Bryan Saussure, two preeminent twenty-first-century scientists, sat on the ground, back to back, looking at him, pleading with their widened eyes. They were gagged! And they appeared to be tied together.

***

By the time Travis realized the screeching voice had stopped addressing the ogre, it was too late for him to even think about fighting back.

His body was briskly whipped around, and before the agent could attempt a struggle, he was flat on his chest while his hands were pinched and then tied behind his back. In another moment, he was whirled around again, until his butt rocked back onto his heels, his knees digging into the stony mud.

This time, Travis found himself face to face with a much smaller creature. Like some impish goblin, the little fiend reached out a long-fingered hand, grasping the agent's face. It scrutinized him carefully, its long-pointed nose and chin leading its eerily intelligent eyes over nearly every speck of the man's head. With a flourish, the imp sneered and then pushed Travis into the waiting paw of the big creature again.

"What do you want with us?" Agent Travis finally managed to sputter in a vain attempt to communicate with the creatures.

The shorter one, obviously the leader, shrieked at him, exposing short, needle-like teeth. Then the ogre backhanded Travis with a fist as big and solid as a frozen turkey, and the agent knew no more.

***

It was a blurry world.

It was a painful world.

It was a moving world. And it was jerky, with a bouncing movement that added to the pain extending through most of his body.

When Agent Travis's eyes finally crept open again, he wanted to put his fingers to his aching head to stop the stabbing pain. But his hands wouldn't cooperate. They wouldn't move at all. Blinking until his vision cleared, he saw the reason. His feet and hands were tightly tied with rough rope to a travois he was strapped to. This primitive pole frame dragged upon the rocky ground, and Travis's body felt every jolt. His head in particular took the brunt of it all, since it was only separated from the ground by bouncing on a rough log.

His legs were four feet above his head, also tied to the poles of the travois. Looking further up, Travis saw the huge, stony hands of the ogre dragging him onward with what appeared to be little effort. And he was gagged by more of that thick, rough rope tied around his head and between his teeth, digging into the corners of his mouth and slowly shredding his lips.

He also noticed they were traveling up a slope. Turning his head to the right, he could look down upon the small open glen and the pond they had come through.

The pond itself was mostly circular in shape, about 50 feet in diameter. Tall stone slabs ringed the pond, much akin to a scaled-back version of Stonehenge. Three of the upright slabs had a horizontal stone laid across their tops.

A portal, Travis thought. *An actual, real portal. So that's what they looked like back in the ancient times.*

Wow, that thought slammed into the agent's brain. *Ancient times. If the professor's calculations were correct, we've gone back to somewhere in the neighborhood of 8,000 years B.C. The time of the receding glaciers. The time when some mythological creatures are more real than imagined.*

A bit behind the monoliths, huge weeping willow trees blocked out the remainder of the deeper forest beyond. Their hanging boughs lent a ghostly appearance to the area around the portal.

About half of the leaves Travis could see were either yellow or steadily changing over from green. *They would be beautifully golden if the sun were out,* Travis thought. *Must be the start of autumn here.*

Painfully turning his head to the left, Travis could see Bryan Saussure and Michael Camaron were tied tightly together on a larger travois that was pulled by a second ogre. Their mouths were gagged just like his. Looking upside-down at the world made it hard to focus.

A third ogre trailed behind them. One hand grasped a large sack that was slung over its shoulder. As far as Agent Travis could tell, these three monsters and the impish creature were the only enemies. Not that it mattered how many enemies there were. The humans weren't likely to escape these captors any time soon.

***

His head pounding in pain, Agent Travis tried to recapture everything that had put the three of them into this current predicament. Considering the rapidity with which he had moved in and out of consciousness recently, it took him a bit.

But he had time. Being a tied prisoner dragged through the wilderness gave him plenty of time to contemplate everything. It seemed easier to start with the present and work backward.

He, the two scientists, and Professor Charles, the aging decades-long leader of the Agency, had been calibrating the time portal's machinery when the building had been attacked. It had likely been the *Brethren*, their old nemesis, though Travis had never known of them ever making such a bold move before.

Michael Camaron and Bryan Saussure had leaped into the portal for safety as the room was being violently destroyed around them. Travis himself was going to "scuttle the ship," so to speak, and sacrifice himself so that Professor Charles could also escape. The technology for time travel could not fall into the hands of the *Brethren*. However, the old man surprised him, as he had on so many occasions over the past 40 years, by pushing Travis into the portal just as the room exploded.

What led up to that fateful day in the Agency's lab, deep beneath the earth's surface?

Decades of collected evidence, supported by archaeology and anthropology, led the Agency to believe in the reality of the ancient Mayans' End of Days prophecy. By 2011, the destruction of the world had been averted four times already, once at the conclusion of each Age of the Sun, approximately every 5,125 years.

Now, our modern world was rolling along the tracks at a breakneck speed toward oblivion. The Fifth Age of the Sun would officially end in December of 2017.

Unfortunately, modern-day cultures long ago lost their connection to the universe's great power source, the "magic" that enabled ancient peoples to prevent each cataclysm or to survive through it.

Without a connection to magic in the world, modern civilizations developed science to best take its place. Shy of scientific advancement, people could only look to divine providence for salvation. Providence or just good luck. Did it really matter which?

Providence had been their savior many times throughout the Agency's history. Numerous times in the past few months, events unfolded that clarified their course of action.

A long-lost Agency explorer who had gone through the portal 20 years ago returned from the distant past. Then a discovery by this esteemed archaeologist Dr. Bryan Saussure changed the entire timeline of the Mayan calendar by almost five years. And a discovery by anthropologist Dr. Michael Camaron demonstrated that a structured human civilization existed in the Great Lakes region as far back as the Ice Age.

And just what was the Agency's role in the world? As a secret arm of the Department of Defense, the Agency investigated instances of preternatural beings and events linked to homeland security. From its earliest creation, the Agency researched deeply into any mythological stories that showed a link to unexplained incidents occurring in our world. Creatures like Bigfoot, Mothman, the Jersey Devil. The Michigan Dogman. Places like Loch Ness, Giza, Bermuda, Ek' Balam, Delphi. There was power and energy in the universe that humans were even now just starting to understand through science.

Mythology is just a relative interpretation of history.

As a grunt in the organization, it would be easy for Travis to take a pragmatic view of his job. A field agent stationed in Michigan, Travis spent the past 40 years tracking a Nagual, known locally as a Dogman, Manwolf, Loup Garou, the Witchy Wolf of the Omer plains, or the Beast of Bray Road outside Elkhorn, Wisconsin.

The creature was believed to be a skinwalker, a type of evil spirit possessing a body that was stuck between human and animal forms. The Dogman wasn't a benign manifestation like most Native stories of shapeshifters. This skinwalker was powerful, malicious, and horrific to behold.

In the time Travis had tracked it, collecting data for the Agency, it had been responsible for the deaths of dozens of humans and countless pets, as well as the destruction of homes, businesses, and even totally wiping out the small village of Sigma.

His job had changed recently, though. He had been pulled from the field, where his protege, Agent Brock, took over tracking the Dogman. Travis had been reassigned to assisting Professor Charles as he assembled a team to prepare and operate the time portal.

We weren't supposed to be here, Travis thought. *We were supposed to send a team of marines and scientists through for this mission.*

Well you're here now, a thought answered him. It had the voice of the old professor. *You're a trained agent, and you're with two scientists. Probably the best two minds on the planet when it comes to understanding what you're up against and how to accomplish your mission.*

What is our mission? Travis asked himself.

What we've talked about this whole last week, came the answer in the professor's voice, and then Travis put all of the pieces together. *Finding out how to stop the cataclysm that will occur at the end of this year in the ancient world in which you're currently residing. And then finding a way back home after gathering as much information as you can that might help us avoid the cataclysm that will occur in 2017. That's what we were sending the team back to do.*

The agent's eyes pivoted back and forth, again taking stock of their current situation. *We might have hit a snag, a little delay in starting up the mission.*

His mind actually played back a couple of seconds of the old professor's soft, grandfatherly chuckle. *You'll find a way. You always do. Concentrate on what you know you can do. Observe everything as if your life depended on it. Because your life does depend on it. Then make a plan. When opportunity arises, make your move and don't hesitate. You can do this.*

***

Their travel came to a sudden halt when the impish creature turned and screeched at its companions. The brutes walking side by side turned their heads toward each other for a moment of understanding, and then they each dropped the travois simultaneously. The humans gave audible groans, even through the ropes that gagged their mouths. The trailing ogre stomped its way up past the others, shoving each in the shoulder as it passed, and dropped the sack it had been carrying. The imp immediately dug through the sack, pulling out chunks of some foul-smelling foodstuff, which it threw at the feet of its larger comrades.

Despite turning his nose up at whatever the creatures were eating, Dr. Saussure's stomach was already grumbling. It seemed ages since they had last eaten breakfast in another world. And they had been dragged for hours since leaving the water portal. Already the light filtering through the gray clouds was diminishing toward the afternoon.

One side of their path appeared to continue rising, dry and rocky, strewn with boulders that likely had rolled their way down from the higher elevations. The other side was forested, though the trees that grew in this dry, stony ground were thin, short, and scraggly with few leaves. Only a few dozen yards ahead, the forest dropped steeply down to a valley, the opening in the trees allowing for what would otherwise be a wonderful view of the landscape for miles around.

The imp went missing for a few minutes into this forested area, but when it reappeared it smacked one of the ogres and led the huge beast over to the humans. The huge, green giant easily plucked up a travois in turn, leaning each one up against a small boulder at the side of the path.

In a quick, agile movement, the small creature pulled the ropes roughly from Michael Camaron's mouth and body, separating him from the travois. His lips were chapped and cut from the gagging ropes, and his wrists, still-tied tightly, were sore and chafed. A second later, the scientist was hefted by the big green brute and carried off out of sight through the knobby, stunted trees that grew along this dry, rocky environment.

Bryan Saussure made eye contact with Agent Travis a few feet away. The good doctor's eyes were in a panic, his head shaking as he contemplated the fate of their companion.

Travis tried to remain calm. He didn't see any reason the monsters would be intentionally harming Michael Camaron at this point. He guessed they had simply stopped for a break in this forced march. If the creatures had wanted to hurt or kill them, they could have done so hours earlier when they were initially captured. They could have done anything they wanted to do to the humans while they were tied up.

They were certainly at the creatures' mercy anyway.

Proving him correct, the ogre returned, carrying their companion, just a few minutes later. Michael Camaron looked none the worse for wear. If anything, he looked refreshed. Before the imp could tie him back up and restore the gag, Michael shared one word with the others: "Water." That put his two companions at ease momentarily, though it brought on a vicious smack across the head from the little goblin creature. A trickle of blood soon snaked its way down along the man's cheek.

Dr. Saussure was taken next. He also returned shortly afterward with a few drops of water on his chin. By the look in his eyes, he was most grateful for the drink. He, however, avoided an extra bashing from the little imp by staying silent as he was rebound.

Finally, it was Agent Travis's turn. He had been looking at every opportunity there might have been for flight these past few minutes. He fully intended to escape when his turn came. But their captor seemed a step ahead of them each time. The procedure was simple and effective.

One captive was released at a time from the travois, though his hands were still tied tightly together. The gag was removed so he could drink. Each human was completely under the control of a giant during the water break. Then the captive was retied to the travois.

As soon as Travis's bonds were freed, that viselike grip was applied to both arms, pinning them against his torso. There would be no escape as long as he was being held. Travis's mind started to search for more options, even as the monster's stony fingers pinched his skin.

Once they left the path, the giant pushed its way through the short trees, easily knocking a few over, and in only a few of its great strides, they had reached a small, shallow creek. Travis's body was uncomfortably tipped upside down as the ogre dipped the agent's head down to the water's cold surface. He drank greedily, holding his breath as most of his face was submerged. Just when he began worrying about the potential for drowning, he was brought back up and they returned to the path to meet up with the rest of the group.

No escape at this point, he thought, disappointed. His mind kept working through scenarios where he wished that he was stronger, quicker, younger, aided with weapons. He looked for the captors to make a mistake but there were none.

***

Out of nowhere, a volley of stones came zipping through the air, pelting the monsters about their heads and faces.

The impish creature brandished his whip, barking orders at the others. Agent Travis, his hands still tied tightly, was dropped in a pile atop his two bound companions, who both groaned behind their gagging ropes. As Travis rolled off the other two, he was kicked in the ribs by a gigantic stony foot. The giant who had dropped him was now standing guard over the travois, its legs like massive, immovable tree trunks on either side of all three humans. Its attention, however, was turned toward its unseen attackers up on the rocky hill instead of the prisoners piled between its ankles.

All of the captors searched the surrounding rocky landscape for their assailants. Cracking his whip overhead, the short goblin-like leader snarled and shrieked some sort of curse at the wilderness. Its pointed, carrot-like nose sniffed the air and its leaf-shaped ears twitched, listening for any sounds of attack. It continued on barking out short bursts of orders to its giant companions.

He was quickly silenced as an arrow slammed into his throat, driving him to the ground. Thick black blood sprayed across the ground. Eyes widened in anguish, the imp clutched at the shaft for a few moments, spitting madly before he expired.

More arrows zipped through the crisp air, striking the giants. There were only nuisances, however. Most of the arrows, even those that targeted their huge, misshapen heads, simply rebounded off the brutes' hardened skin. The few arrows that did manage to penetrate did no real damage. These few simply stuck out at various angles, like quills on an angry porcupine.

Unharmed, the gigantic beasts turned toward the boulder-strewn hill from whence the projectiles came. They snarled upward, slowly searching for their assailants.

***

While the enemies were otherwise engaged, Travis kept wriggling his hands, trying to loosen the ties. If there was a chance at escape, it was now, while the giants were distracted.

Unable to make any headway with his own bands, the agent scooted his back up against Bryan Saussure's, since he was the closest. The good doctor, panicking as usual, was little help. His hands may have been tied, but they fidgeted and interfered with Travis's attempts.

"Hold still!" Travis, the only one who hadn't been regagged, hissed quietly over his shoulder, trying not to be overheard by their guard above them.

But then the agent paused, as a resounding war cry pierced the otherwise still air. He lifted his head and eyes and took his own turn looking around to see what new predicament they had been thrown into.

The battle was on.

Chapter 2

A powerfully built native leapt down from his hidden position about 30 paces up the trail at the head of a narrow, rocky ravine that cut across their path and fell steeply away from the thin, spidery woods. He crouched low to the ground, his body nimbly rocking back and forth. His feet were covered by moccasins made of thongs interlaced around his toes and ankles. A simple, one-piece leather tunic covered most of his torso, loosely flowing halfway to his knees. Around his waist was tied a rope belt in which a couple of small pouches and stone tools clung close to his body.

The giants roared in anger, and the two closest charged ahead, their thudding feet echoing along the boulders. Their huge war clubs swung back and forth, ready for action.

The native didn't flinch. In the breeze, his long, thin black hair streamed back behind his tanned face. His dark eyes never left the rushing attackers.

"NEE-HAI!" came another war cry as the two giants neared their target. Only a second or two before impact, another native, a near twin to the first, flew feet-first through the air.

His powerful kick caught the first ogre just beneath the left armpit. Really the only vulnerable spot, this impact didn't injure the huge creature, though it did knock it off balance.

Spun out of control, the first giant toppled sideways and rolled to the stony earth. The second giant, unable to stop its momentum or change its direction, tumbled right over its companion and splayed out flat on the ground.

Both of their weapons bounced out of their huge hands, and were further tossed away by the pair of quick–thinking natives.

Travis returned his attention to escaping. He still tried to move slowly and not draw attention to himself and what he was doing. The guards, however, took no notice of their captives. Their full concentration had turned to whoever was assaulting them.

***

The third ogre scowled at the scene unfolding up the path. Its tiny brain couldn't quite decide whether to rush into the battle, as it wanted desperately to do, or to stay and guard the prisoners, as it had been commanded to.

This indecision cost the creature its life. From behind, the giant was knocked to the ground by yet another attacker, whose well-placed kick caught it right below the shoulder blades.

Travis didn't get a chance to see it happen, but he did see the eyes of his two companions widen in surprise and fear as their beastly captor fell to its knees with a thud, just missing their heads. The impact of several hundred pounds of monster would have likely crushed their skulls.

Without hesitation, this third native, surprisingly agile, landed upon the creature's wide back. She slammed down the shaft of her mighty spear with a strength that would have skewered a wild boar.

The sharpened point pierced the giant's skin where the neck met the shoulder. Death was instantaneous.

Michael Camaron watched the attack in awe. It all happened so quickly, so perfectly timed.

And despite the danger all around them, the complete uncertainty of whether these three newcomers were allies or enemies, Michael was instantly and totally captivated by this woman who had leapt into their lives.

He was mesmerized by the woman's beauty, the grace of her movements, the silent savagery of her attack.

Agent Travis rolled out of the way. In one smooth, fluid motion the woman swung her stone blade and sliced easily through the rough ropes that bound the men together. Another few seconds and each was completely free.

***

The two giants didn't stay on the ground very long. They had not yet noticed their dead comrade behind them. And neither of them was interested in the captives who had been freed and had followed the native woman into hidden spots in the trees.

Instead, they were both standing back up, furiously looking for their assailants, who had since disappeared.

A few seconds later, the assault continued once again.

This time, an avalanche of boulders rumbled down the hillside. They weren't huge by any means, but the landslide of smaller debris caused unstable footing as the giants tried to step around the larger, knee-high boulders.

As the giants were distracted by the rubble, a hook-shaped bone affixed to a long rope came darting out of the wilderness, aimed at the head of the nearest ogre. This grappling tool wound its way around one of the giant's horns, securing itself tightly against the rope to which it was tied.

The warrior who threw it immediately sprinted up the edge of the half-moon ravine, pulling the rope tightly as he ran. His momentum snapped the giant's head back as the native completed his mad dash around the ravine. He pulled backward with all of his might as he crossed the path ahead.

Losing its balance, the ogre spun and tumbled, still slipping on the loose pebbles. And then, it suddenly went over the edge.

The native man let loose the rope with a cry of victory. Arms flailing and reaching where no handhold was to be found, the monster gave a surprised howl as its balance was lost and it plummeted down the steep hill, caroming off of rocks and uprooting trees on its way to the bottom, several hundred feet below. A cloud of dust puffed up, obscuring the creature's final landing spot.

Emboldened by this success, the other warrior slung his grappling rope at the other giant to repeat the attack. But that ogre was ready for it. The monster reached one gigantic hand up and caught the bone hook. With a tremendous tug, it yanked the warrior off his feet and all the way across the path.

The creature's other fist swing forward, smashing into the native's head with a sickening crunch. The man's broken body went limp immediately in mid-air, well before it redirected off the sharp boulders at the side of the path.

The warrior woman screamed in anguish, leaping from her hidden spot among the trees. Tears already starting to run from her eyes, she charged up the path toward the enemy, belting out her war cry. Her face was a grimacing mask of hatred and pain.

The last remaining ogre turned sideways, trying to see the attacks that were coming at it from both ends of the path. It prepared to swing its massive fist at the woman who would reach it first.

But just before impact she abruptly dropped down below its punch and between the creature's legs. The monster's legs buckled as the other native kicked it from behind, high up on its back.

The woman safely popped up on the other side, but then she gasped as she watched the monster grasp the warrior's leg just as it slipped over the edge of the cliff. The warrior gave one last surprised look at the woman before both man and beast disappeared a fraction of a second later.

She ran to the edge and dropped to her knees, wailing for her lost companion, whose body was seen unmoving, bloody and badly impaled on a sharp tree branch halfway down the steep hillside. Her hands alternated between covering her weeping face and then angrily grasping her long, black hair.

This second giant crashed through the pine branches far below, coming to rest not too far from its comrade.

***

The three time travelers couldn't understand a word the native woman was saying as she grieved over her lost companions. But it was obvious that they needed to leave quickly.

Agent Travis and Michael Camaron looked down over the ravine's edge. As the dust was finally settling a hundred feet below, they could see the two giants were merely stunned, not dead as they had hoped. Robust arms and legs were pushing off the layer of rubble as they slowly freed themselves.

"I've got the feeling," Travis said quietly, "that somehow they'll find a way back up. It might take them a while, but they'll get back up here."

"Yeah," Camaron whispered back. "And I don't want to be anywhere near here when they do."

Travis nodded. "I think we should get moving. Somewhere, anywhere but here."

In the meantime, their new ally was pulling the body of the fallen warrior far back into the half-moon-shaped notch in the hillside. She removed two of the ribbons from her arms and tied them gently across the dead man's eyes. Then she used her stone knife to begin cutting into the dry, stony ground.

She spoke not a word, but tears ran in little rivulets down her darkly tanned face.

Digging the grave was painstakingly slow work, and it was painful to watch her. At one point, Michael Camaron tried to help her, but she pushed him away vehemently, hissing words at him.

"I think she needs to complete this ritual herself," Bryan Saussure said slowly.

The other two time travelers looked incredulously at the good doctor. "You can understand her?" Camaron asked.

As the woman continued the preparations for the simple burial plot, she spoke softly to herself, almost in a chanting or singing manner. Bryan cocked his head slightly, listening intently.

"It's not an exact match," he said to his companions, "but the language she's speaking is very similar to the ancient Nahuatl, the parent-tongue to the language spoken by the Mayans and later the Aztecs. I think she's asking the great spirit to accept the souls of these departed warriors. This one here I think was her mate." He nodded toward the cliff. "I think the other one, down there, was her brother."

Still, the native woman continued to dig in the dry, stony ground.

As soon as the trench was as long as the body and about two feet deep, she tugged the dead warrior into position. Gently, she caressed his hands and cheeks, and kissed his forehead. Then she prayed over him in whispers no one else could hear.

When she was finished with the ritual, she said something urgently in her language, pointing first at the time travelers and then at the rocks and stones that littered the edge of the path.

"Collect the stones," Dr. Saussure did his best to translate. "She wants us to gather the stones for her."

Travis nodded to his companions. "Then let's get these rocks for her. The faster we help her build the cairn, the faster we can get out of here."

The three quickly scavenged the path and before long they had a heap of stones piled next to the body. The native woman meticulously placed each stone, taking considerable time in the process.

While Michael and Bryan solemnly watched the funeral, Agent Travis reported from the edge of the ravine. "They're fully awake, trying to climb their way back up. It'll be awhile yet, I'm sure. But if we can get moving, I think we can put some miles between us."

Finally, the cairn was completed. The mound was about a foot and a half high when she was finished.

The last thing she did was to collect dry, dead branches to cover everything, doing her best to make it all blend in so no one would necessarily know they had been there and disturb the warrior's resting place.

***

She grasped her spear, which was still sticking out of the ogre's neck. With one mighty tug, she violently pulled it from the creature's body.

Then she snarled, seeming to take pleasure in stabbing the dead little goblin creature. With the sharp end of her spear, she flung its body over the cliff edge and down atop the two giants below.

It was barely a distraction as one of the brutes just flicked the imp's body out of its way. Then the warrior woman cursed for several seconds in her language and spit savagely in their direction. Finally, she closed her eyes and quietly chanted a prayer over the body of her brother far below.

Agent Travis looked back at the others from where he was standing ahead on the path. "We should get going. Who knows when reinforcements might arrive."

The warrior woman pointed her spear up the rocky hillside and then began carefully climbing.

"She wants us to go this way," Bryan said.

Michael Camaron shrugged his shoulders. "I'm sticking with her. If we run into any more of these thugs, I want to be on her side."

Moments later, all three of the time travelers were scaling their way into the wilderness.

***

Within a few hours, Dr. Saussure was able to communicate with the woman in a rudimentary manner. He was correct that the language she spoke was fundamentally similar to those languages he had been studying in the Yucatan.

As they hiked, Bryan stayed close to her, continuously posing questions to her and carefully filing away the vocabulary she used for everything from environmental structures to animals to the weather.

At first she seemed annoyed by his persistent, systematic questions. Then she seemed resigned that perhaps this was just the way this strange, pale human acted, speaking as if he hadn't a clue as to the name of anything in her world.

Only a few times did they stop to rest, and always near a water source. The small creeks ran with cold, clear, delicious water, and at each they all drank their fill.

At one of their breaks, Bryan stepped aside to speak privately with his two companions. "Her name is Rio," the good doctor explained. "Pronounced like the river, or the city in Brazil. Or at least that's the closest I can pronounce it. She rolls the long 'e' sound in a peculiar fashion."

"You two have been talking up quite a storm," Michael said. "Have you been able to learn anything about her? About this world?"

"She confirmed it was her husband and her brother who were killed freeing us," Bryan said. "Her husband was the one she buried."

"Wow," Michael sighed. "I guess that explains a lot. I can't imagine having to just up and leave them the way she did. She's got us on quite a march. Does she believe we're in danger?"

Bryan nodded. "I haven't quite gotten around to that level of questioning yet. But yes, I can tell she's on alert. Constantly. She regularly tells me to speak quieter, and I see her head always darting around."

"I was thinking we should introduce ourselves since we have a moment. What do you think?" Bryan asked.

Agent Travis nodded. "We're all going to need to learn as much of her language as possible, as quickly as possible. She's the only link we have to this world. She seems to feel we have some importance for her to have saved us in the first place and then to lead us away from danger. I think the sooner we are all on speaking terms, the better."

Rio was sharpening the ends of her spear with a flat, palm-sized rock when the three time travelers knelt down by her.

Dr. Saussure led them through a simple yet polite introduction, using the best etiquette he could muster from what he knew about Yucatan customs. It worked. Within a minute, Rio could identify each of them by name, though the best she could pronounce them was: Bray-en, Mi-gel, and Trah-vis.

***

As night fell, Rio called a halt where a thick copse of fir trees grew tightly against an outcropping of stone. It was the best location for shelter and safety that any of the three time travelers had seen so far.

Under Rio's directions, they gathered firewood of all different sizes. She produced two small stones from the pouch at her waist and after only a couple of seconds of striking, a small flame emerged from the kindling. Very carefully she added in a piece at a time to ensure the fire stayed low and produced almost no smoke.

All four were very hungry, but there was nothing to eat. As the temperature dropped quickly, the world around them dimmed to complete blackness. They all huddled closely together around the fire, shivering slightly in spite of the warmth of the flames.

"Are you able to talk more with her yet?" Agent Travis asked the good doctor. "Ask her about those creatures? Find out more about this world?"

"And why they snagged us so quickly after we came through the portal," Michael said.

Bryan began speaking to Rio, adding in hand gestures and sometimes seeming to frown and backtrack through his own words. The time travelers had many questions.

At first, the woman answered in individual short bursts of words. But the more they talked, she seemed to open up and provided them with the longer, more complete answers they were seeking. Bryan Saussure gained more confidence in his linguistic skills the more he continued to speak with her.

"It appears these evil creatures were waiting for us," Bryan translated. "She says the portal we crossed through has been guarded constantly for many moons. The big, horned giants she calls *Bergrisar* and the smaller, goblin-like creature she calls a *Maugwat*. The *Bergrisar* are mainly servants, huge stupid creatures. They're the thugs that do the dirty work. The *Maugwat* was in charge. That's why they killed it first."

"She says they were taking us as prisoners to a dark place. I don't quite understand that part yet, but I get the feeling it isn't someplace pleasant. She keeps using the name *Xoloctil*. I know that's a close rendition of what we call the name of the mythological Mayan god of the underworld. But could that really be the case?"

Michael sighed. "Considering everything we've learned about the mythological history of our world in the past few weeks. And now that we're seeing living proof of creatures, I'd believe just about anything at this point."

"She and the other two warriors have also been watching the portal," Bryan said. "She had a dream, a vision, that she says came from their gods. She claims our arrival was foretold by part of their mythology. Pale-skinned men would arrive through the portal. They'd come unarmed into this world, but they were really great warriors in disguise."

Bryan stopped a moment and looked directly at his companions across the fire. "She says we've come to stop the spreading darkness and to save the world."

They all fell silent for a time, before Dr. Saussure continued. "There's more. Her dream indicated they were supposed to escort us to the mountains where we would find and lead a great army into battle. Rio is bound by her oath to her dead husband and brother to protect us on this journey."

***

The foursome struck out for the high country. Over the next three days, they moved continuously and steadily uphill.

Rio proved a magnanimous traveling companion. She moved quickly but surefooted in the wilderness. And while they didn't stop to hunt, she was a great forager, easily finding enough food for the four of them. It wasn't extravagant, but it was enough to survive upon.

Bryan Saussure became more and more fluent in her language. He also began teaching the others, though Agent Travis had far more difficulty in picking it up than Michael Camaron did.

On the fourth afternoon since their liberation, the thick gray cloud cover began dissipating, and by dusk the time travelers saw the first pinpoints of starlight in this ancient world.

With the clear sky, the temperatures dropped significantly. Once again, Rio started a small warm fire that provided enough heat without the smoke that could draw the attention of any enemies.

"Did you notice the stars?" Michael asked Travis. "They're different than our sky. The constellations are different."

Michael pointed upward. "That star...follow my finger...it's not super bright. I'm going to make the assumption that's Polaris, the North Star. It's roughly in the right location, but not exactly, and it does curve down into the Little Dipper, though it curves the wrong way. But if you backtrack, there's no Big Dipper to point at it."

Travis really had little point of reference for the stars. His attention had always been on events unfolding here on earth rather than in space. He could only take Michael's description of this ancient sky as accurate.

Bryan, on the other hand, was versed in enough astronomy to tie in with his deep knowledge of mythology. He could easily see what Michael Camaron was pointing out in the heavens, and he nodded in agreement.

Michael continued, "You can also see most of Draco, which is interesting, because of the way this dragon constellation curves to its last star, called Thuban. It was theorized that Thuban was the polar star thousands of years before Polaris took its place."

"That's correct," Dr. Saussure added, "You know, the pole stars revolve approximately every 26,000 years." He also pointed up, nearly directly overhead. "If you look up in that same relative location, you can see three stars in roughly a triangle. Polaris, Thuban, and that one is Vega from the modern-day Lyra constellation. Those three stars take turns at aligning as the north celestial pole every couple of thousand years.

"We're only spitballing here, and we're without a compass to tell us which way is north for sure, but based on the location of these three stars, I would guess we are someplace between 6,000 and 9,000 years B.C. My best guess anyway."

Travis nodded. "Pretty good reasoning, doctor. The portal machinery was set for the year 8240 B.C. That was the year Professor Charles calculated for the end of the Third Age of the Sun."

"Yes, the end of 13 B'ak'tuns in the long-count calendar. I guess we're really here, aren't we," Bryan stated more than asked.

Chapter 3

Another long day of hiking. Another day with very little to eat. Another evening sitting around a campfire with a grumbling belly.

Agent Travis did his best to distract himself from hunger pangs by recalling events in his past. As he looked around at his companions, he could only shake his head and wonder how indeed they all ended up here. Was it karma? Was it simple coincidence?

Or like Professor Charles believed, was there indeed a higher power at work, a power that could occasionally ensnare an innocent passerby who had a unique set of abilities and put that person into a situation where something truly great could occur?

Travis wasn't religious by any sort of the imagination. He didn't know if he believed in God, at least any god in particular. But he did believe in a higher power, like the professor did.

If that power was tied with a deity, then so be it. If it was simply the natural energy of the universe that could be harnessed by the occasional innocent passerby, then so be it. If it was just like the "Force" of Obi Wan Kenobi, then so be it.

Here he sat, an aging man with a unique subset of abilities, most of them in the sphere of observation.

Across the campfire from him sat a mysterious warrior, his counterpart really, who appeared to have more experiences than all three combined.

On either side of him sat two fairly impressive scientific minds with their own specific talents.

They were indeed an interesting company.

And yes, they each seemed to have been ensnared by some higher power, tossed together like dice in a cup, ready to roll with whatever circumstance arose.

He thought about Dr. Saussure's reaction when they were attacked on Lake Michigan. It was hard to believe that was barely more than a week ago. Bryan had spent most of the time below decks green with seasickness. And when the shooting started, Bryan followed orders just well enough to ensure his own safety.

Now, here that eminent scientist was, an integral component in their company, a man whose background in linguistics made it possible to communicate effectively with the native population.

And then there was Michael Camaron. He was an overgrown Boy Scout. Explorer, naturalist, academic, lover of the outdoors. He was the counterpart to Bryan Saussure.

Travis watched Michael, who was fiddling with the necklace and pendant he wore just beneath the collar of his now-faded red polo shirt.

That shirt was bright red when we crossed over, Travis thought. *Now you can barely even see the embroidered University of Wisconsin logo on it. His cargo shorts have held up fairly well. But his Brewers cap must have disappeared in the portal the way my jacket, tie, and Glock all did.* He sighed. *Sometimes I really miss that pistol.*

The necklace and pendant reminded Agent Travis of the silver chain and amulet he had given to his partner, Agent Brock, when they had parted ways. Like so many events, that seemed so long ago and yet it was only days before they had entered the portal.

Agent Brock had been assigned to take Travis's place in the field. Travis believed that the kid would need all the help he could get in tracking his own Nagual through Northern Michigan. The amulet had saved Travis's life from the Dogman. He had given it to Brock hoping it might save his life someday, too.

Little did Travis think back then that he might have a better use for it. Of course, he wouldn't have dreamed in a million years that he'd be living in the Nagual's ancient world, a place where that amulet might have been quite a source of power indeed.

No matter, he thought. *The amulet is with Brock in the modern day Upper Peninsula. Wishing for it here won't do any good, so don't bother.*

"What is that necklace you're wearing?" Agent Travis asked Michael around the side of the fire.

Michael displayed a square charm. It was about an inch on each side and appeared to be made of a yellowish stone. A pattern of lines was lightly carved into it.

"My grandfather gave this to me. He found it in the southwest, where he was on a dig in the Pueblo country back, oh, probably more than 50 years ago. He was an anthropologist, too," Michael said with a half smile.

Bryan looked up. "I thought you were a climatologist."

Michael took his eyes off his charm. "That's just my current job. But my passion has always been anthropology. My grandfather was my inspiration. He was the reason I study ancient cultures, too. He found this charm deeply buried in a *cavate*, an ancient cliff cave dwelling."

Staring into the embers, Michael continued, "No one really knows why the cliff dwellers built their cities tucked back into the overhanging mesas. The Pueblo are some of the most ancient people in all of the U.S. And they're unlike so many of the other tribes in the southwest. They seem to have more in common with the peoples of Central America than with their neighbors just around them.

"My grandfather often found it ironic that the Pueblo had so much in common with modern Americans. They built their homes in multiple levels, with many smaller rooms. The cliff dwellings were like apartment buildings.

"It's almost as if someone from the future had gone back in time to design their dwellings based on far more modern-day architecture. And many of them were built thousands of years ago. Even carbon-dating methods aren't reliable, because it's all made of sand and rock."

"You're more right than you know," Dr. Saussure interjected. "That's because their ancestors, the Anasazi, have many links to the cultures of Meso-America. There are many in my field, myself included, who believe they all share common ancestors."

Michael looked around at his companions, smiling. "Did you know that most of the cliff dwellers only chose caves that faced the west or southwest? No one really seems to know why. Or even why they built those elaborate villages completely within the protection of the overarching plateau."

"You said it yourself," Agent Travis mused. "For protection."

"But protection from what?" Michael answered. "They were warriors. Their artifacts show better military technology than any other tribes in their locale."

"Maybe it was something besides other humans. Maybe there was an issue in their environment."

"It's a mystery we'll likely never have an answer to. We'll certainly never find out while we're in this world."

"Do you think there's a way back?" Dr. Saussure asked.

Agent Travis continued staring at the small flames. "There is a way."

The others looked to him expectantly. In a few moments, Travis went on. "We always knew we could send someone through our constructed portal. And we knew that...things...could come back through natural portals into our world. But the portal our agency created was unable to provide two-way access."

Travis slowly stirred the embers with a stick until little teeth of fire poked upward. "Professor Charles theorized that portals might really only allow travel in one direction. Of course, he couldn't prove it."

"But you said there is a way back," Dr. Saussure pressed.

Travis sighed. "We'd have to find a portal here that corresponded with our own time period."

"I don't like those odds," Michael said.

"Well, they're slightly better than you might think," Travis answered. "Though still a long shot. You see, a few months ago, one of our agents returned to our world after being gone for nearly 20 years. He was a part of the original experiments. Back then, when we couldn't bring him back, we were resigned to believing that he was gone for good. Then in March, just weeks ago, he suddenly appeared in the far western end of the Upper Peninsula."

"And what did he say?"

Frowning, Travis said, "Agent Mitchell died of exposure before we could retrieve any information from him. But in the week before we crossed over, we did send an agent to the Upper Peninsula on a mission to find that portal. It hardly seems to have been only, what, 10 days ago?"

Bryan sounded hopeful. "But that does prove that there's a portal, somewhere in this world, a portal that connects back. We just have to find it."

Michael gave a cursory glance around them. "Where should we start?"

"I don't know," Travis answered. "But we need to keep our eyes open at all times for clues." Travis nodded toward Rio. "Maybe she will be of help to us, too. Professor Charles believed that the entire world, the existence of all of us, spins around one great epic tale. He called it 'Theoretical Storytelling' and connected it to the bigger picture of what it means to be a human species and to be alive in a world that is alive with many other species. To interact with and to understand the place of all these species in the great tale of the world."

"And some of those species are what we refer to as monsters, beasts, even deities?" asked Bryan.

"That's how Professor Charles saw the world," replied Travis.

"And what do you think, agent?" Michael asked.

Travis paused. "I've seen so many things that defy understanding. Creatures that came to life right out of legends. Scientific advancements that might as well be considered magic. And here we are, in the ancient past. The professor always said things happen for a reason. Stories are passed on through the generations, the centuries, for a reason."

"You've studied mythology, doctor," Michael said to Dr. Saussure. "Think about the connections between the mythologies of cultures all around the world and from all different time periods. There are hundreds of common threads between them, from specific characters to specific events. Take the great flood, the 'leviathan' creature, epic journeys, heroes who are sacrificed for their tragic flaws, trickster characters. These are the same the world over."

Michael paused, then said softly, "Or the concept of werewolves. That Nagual creature I saw in the virtual reality machine was worse than any story, any horror movie I ever saw."

Rio's head jerked up at the name "Nagual," though the three men didn't notice her reaction.

"You've seen it, right?" Michael asked Travis.

Travis stared into the fire for a long time before answering. "Yes. From a distance a few times and twice up close and personally. Tracking that beast has consumed most of my life. So many questions and so few answers. Every time we learn more about the beast, hundreds of more questions arose."

"Just another species in the great tale of the world, huh?" Michael responded.

"The problem with this species," Travis continued, "is it's trying to end the world. According to Professor Charles, the Dogmen periodically try to do that. They seem to show up at the end of each Age of the Sun. It makes them not only highly dangerous but also incredibly inconvenient if they're not stopped."

Rio broke her silence and began speaking rapidly. Bryan listened carefully, responded a few times, and then translated for them.

"She says the Nagual, the Dogmen, are the personal minions of Xoloctil. They are his bodyguards and the backbone of his armies. They were created by the darkest magic, transforming the most evil men into foul creatures. There is little that can be done to stop these foul creatures and almost nothing that can kill them."

Bryan listened more and then continued. "She also says the Nagual are moving through the land again. There are tales of them leading roving bands of dark, human marauders across the central plains and throughout the northlands. They're killing off all who resist them and leading those who will join their ranks on the side of evil."

"Doesn't sound too promising," Michael remarked dryly.

Obstacles in the path of our mission, thought Travis. *Some pretty big obstacles... with long claws and fangs.*

***

When the sun was an arm's length from being directly overhead on their fifth day of hiking, the travelers encountered the first vestiges of a civilization from this time period.

Unfortunately, it had been already destroyed.

Rio had been noticeably excited the entire morning, ever since they had set out from the night's resting spot. She had spoken more over those couple of hours than most of their previous days of travel put together.

Dr. Saussure continued his translations, but even Michael and Travis could pick up the warrior woman's buoyancy.

She said they were approaching a village, one that held a special place in her heart.

Dr. Saussure did his best, as always, to translate her language, especially when she spoke quickly and with emotion. "She calls them the *Nesatin*," Bryan said. "She doesn't quite indicate this place is her home, but she sure seems to have a strong connection to the place and its people. It appears she's spent considerable time there."

When the treeline opened up and they had stepped into a large clearing, they all realized that civilization would not flourish in this spot for a long time to come.

***

Saying there was almost nothing left of the Nesatin village would be almost an understatement.

Dozens of black, burned-out areas were all that was left of the lodges. Other than these pyres, the clearing was flat and void of anything that resembled human artifacts or remains.

Rio staggered into the edge of the village proper, completely devastated by the scene before her. After only a couple of steps, her knees buckled and she nearly dropped to the ground.

Slight tendrils of smoke wafted up from the remnants of a couple of pyres. Michael Camaron thought the entire village looked as if it was part of an old black-and-white horror movie, like the classics he grew up watching at midnight on Saturday nights.

In a daze, Rio moved, ghostlike, from one burned-out pyre to another. Her face was aghast in utter disbelief. She mumbled bits of phrases in her own language. Dr. Saussure stayed just close enough to her to listen and do his best to translate for the others.

The three time travelers felt sick, and not just from the underlying acrid stench around them. They all felt an uneasiness deep within their stomachs. This wasn't just a battle; it was an extermination.

In his college days, Michael Camaron had taken several Native American history classes. He had read of the accounts of tribes battling each other, of feuds between villages. Even when tribes declared war upon each other, only in rare instances was everyone in a village killed.

Usually the victors would take women and children as slaves, sometimes adopting them into their own families.

The worst instances usually involved the U.S. Cavalry sweeping in and killing every inhabitant. But even the Cavalry didn't completely eradicate every single artifact of the native's existence.

The three men watched Rio continue to slowly drift from one side of the ruined village to the other. Her face was as ashen as the gray dust that drifted up from her footfalls.

Bryan Saussure knelt down near the one ash pile that was still smoking. He reached his hand out over the ashes. Agent Travis and Michael watched him closely. "It's not warm, but it's not cold either."

"This just recently happened," Michael whispered. "Maybe last night? Certainly not more than a day ago. It's hard to judge by the air temperature."

"Do you feel it?" Bryan asked, and Michael nodded. "It feels like we're being watched."

Agent Travis looked to the treeline around the ruined village. "We need to leave. Now."

At that moment, the silence was broken by the crackling of a stick at the edge of the treeline. All four spun, preparing themselves for the worst.

***

Out of the woods stumbled a small girl. She appeared to be maybe three or four years old. Her body was filthy, her skin smeared with black grime.

She staggered toward them, limping badly on what might have been a broken ankle or leg. A trail of blood ran down the left side of her head from beneath her hair and was plastered to her scalp. Beneath a series of bruises, only one of her eyes was barely open enough to see through.

The child made it only a few steps into the clearing before Rio sprinted to her. The warrior woman arrived just as the child tripped and was about to hit the ground. Rio caught her in both arms and cradled her to her chest, carefully crouching to the ground.

The three men were just a few seconds behind. As they crowded around, they picked up bits and pieces of the mostly one-sided conversation. Rio carefully smoothed out the child's hair, pulling it back from her face and tucking it behind her grimy ears as she slowly and calmly spoke to the little girl.

Bryan Saussure translated everything that the other two couldn't understand.

"It appears she's the only survivor here," Bryan whispered. "Her name is Tepin. They were attacked by an army of dark men, covered in furs like bears or wolves. Her mother told her to hide beneath the sleeping skins when their home collapsed, trapping them inside. She managed to dig herself out as the lodge burned around her. She crawled through the burning village to the woods, where she has been hidden since."

The little girl softly groaned in pain, her bruised left hand raising her fingers to touch the head injury that was still oozing dark red blood. Her face grimaced in pain though she didn't seem to have the energy to cry out.

Rio held her and rocked her gently, softly singing to her in a barely audible voice. As she whispered the lullaby, the girl's eyes closed one last time, now forever, her life force having slipped away.

***

The three men endured Rio preparing another shallow grave, this time in the soft earth of the clearing beyond the burned areas of the Nesatin village itself. Like the time before, Rio wouldn't let them help her. When she finished the task, the clouds overhead had thickened and darkened again.

They had all returned back among the pyres, looking for more clues as to what had happened here. Everything was apparently burned—the people, their tools, their homes, everything.

Then Michael saw something out of the corner of his eye. His head whipped around. "What is that?" he croaked, his voice barely audible. Without intending, he'd reached out and clutched Bryan's forearm. When the good doctor turned, he just about jumped out of his skin.

Out of the tendrils of smoke, a ghost-like form began to materialize, floating several feet above the scorched earth. It was a transparent-gray color, like the ashes spread throughout the ruined village.

There were partial legs that ended at about where knees should have been. Long, wispy arms extended from its torso.

As this phantom separated itself from the smoldering smoke, details of its face began to sharpen. A dark cavity drooped open where its mouth should have been. Tiny golden lights blazed in its otherwise hollow eye sockets.

The entire clearing was silent. Dead silent. No wind, no birds. And suddenly the four humans all felt frigid, as if the temperature had instantly dropped 20 or 30 degrees. Goose pimples covered their arms, legs, necks, any exposed skin. The very air itself seemed to have become thickened, taking on a pale, yellowish tint.

All four travelers found themselves quickly packed together in a tight group a few paces away. Rio and Travis backed slowly away from the apparition, while Bryan and Michael peeked around their sides.

"There's another one!" Bryan whispered loudly, pointing to their left.

"Another one here, too," Michael added, looking to their right.

Indeed nearly a dozen of these specters were now visible, ever so slowly encircling the humans.

"Keep moving backward," Agent Travis commanded. "We need to get clear of the village."

More and more of the ghosts slowly rose from the burned out pyres. Those who had appeared first now took on facial features that resembled humans in agony. Ghastly, translucent skin showed how they died, most with massive burns or deep lacerations.

Rio spoke several choppy sentences that only Bryan could understand. "She says we must not let them touch us. The power of the dead in this world is strong. Very strong. They are disturbed because they were not buried properly and now they cannot move on to the next world. They hate us because we are living. They'll do anything to get their revenge on the living."

"But we didn't cause this!" Michael nearly shouted, both to his companions and to the phantoms around them. "We didn't kill them."

"They don't know that," Bryan said. "I don't think they care. And I don't think they quite communicate with us either way."

While their expressions made the apparitions look lost, the tiny eye lights focused on the mortals with a deadly fixation. It was a look that placed the full blame of their deaths on the hands of the living.

Michael and Bryan plotted a course in and around the charred remains of the village, doing their best to keep as far a distance from the ghosts as possible.

Travis was right on their heels.

Rio had her spear up at shoulder level, pointing it outward to ward off the specters whose arms were reaching out toward the humans.

Finally, Michael could see a break in the ever-crowded field of phantoms and that gap ran back toward the forest. "I see the way out!" he yelled. "Run!"

All four sprinted, their breath puffing out white clouds in the blooming frigid air that had descended upon the ruined village. Ghosts on each side moved to intercept the mortals before they could escape.

The living and the dead converged on a single point. Michael, Bryan, and Travis all slipped through before the specters could touch them.

Rio, the last in line, was not quite as lucky. The slender, wispy arms of two ghosts reached out to grasp the woman. Her momentum carried her through the boundary of the desolation, her chest and upper arms passing directly through the phantom appendages.

She ran on a few long strides before nose-diving to the ground.

***

Agent Travis was the first to notice, and he yelled at the other two men ahead of him. They doubled back, grasped Rio and dragged her fully inside the treeline.

Already, the temperature seemed to rise. Their breathing no longer created little puffs of vapor. Looking back, Bryan saw the ghosts of the Nesatin village already dissipating just as the cloud cover overhead did the same.

Rio's body, however, was ice-cold around the chest and arms. She was unconscious and her breathing was shallow.

Immediately, Michael dropped to the ground and wrapped his arms around her, hugging her tightly against his torso.

"Let's get a fire going," Agent Travis said. "We need to warm her body up quickly." He and Bryan wasted no time in gathering materials. It took them far longer to strike the woman's firestones together and produce a spark that would grow into a flame. But they eventually managed it.

Within a few minutes, Rio stirred in her sleep. When her eyelids fluttered open, she glanced up into the face of Michael Camaron, who still held her securely. Despite their relative inability to understand words in each other's language, there was plenty of communication occurring as they stared into each other's eyes.

"We can't stay here long," Bryan said, still stealing glances up at the destroyed village, fully expecting to see an army of ghosts ready to attack them. The charred remains, however, were still and silent.

Travis had also been looking back. "It looks pretty calm now. But I don't want to be around here after night falls. How's she doing?" he asked Michael.

The young scientist gave a slight smile, his eyes still not leaving her face. "She's going to be just fine. Just a little longer to rest and regain her strength."

Rio's eyes closed softly as she slipped back into sleep. They let her rest for what the men felt was about two more hours, or what she had taught them were two arm lengths of the sun's crossing in the sky. Then Michael awakened her gently, and they left without another glance back at the ruined village.

***

The company pushed on as quickly as they could, wishing desperately to put some great distance between themselves and the horror back at the Nesatin village. None of them really thought the phantoms would leave the general area in which they had been killed as humans. But none of them really wanted to find out for sure either.

About an arm's length of the sun's journey away from the ruins of the village, the forest opened up into a wide meadow. Bryan guessed it was a mile long and maybe half a mile wide.

The golden-green grass was waist high and thick. Not fully trusting such an open area, or what could be hidden low in the grass, the travelers stayed close to the treeline. About halfway around the meadow, the sun peeked out of the clouds and illuminated the landscape. Everywhere, wildflowers bloomed in a rainbow of colors, a scene of truly breathtaking beauty.

There wasn't time to stop and bask in the beauty of the natural world, however. They felt compelled to keep pushing on, not only because that had become their custom since first following Rio, but also to be as far from that ruined village as possible. Not one of them felt they could get far enough away to prevent the nightmares they were sure would occur in the wee hours of the night.

Finally, with darkness nearly upon them, they stopped. Rio fell asleep by the fire just after she got it started. That left the other three scavenging in the woods for their own dinners. They were still hungry when darkness completely fell and instead of filling their bellies, they settled around the campfire for safety and warmth.

The three time travelers stared into the flames. Around them, the noises of insects and an occasional call of a bird filled the space beneath the tree canopy.

"Now she blames herself for the destruction at the village as well as the deaths of her mate and her brother," Bryan whispered. "I could pick up some of that when she mumbled in her sleep this afternoon."

"I seemed to pick up some of it, too," Michael agreed. "More the feelings than the words themselves. That's a burden no one should have to take on. What happened to them wasn't her fault."

Bryan sighed. "She believes she deserved the pain she received from the ghost's touch. She seems to think that if either of the two warriors who helped rescue us had lived, if she had protected even one of them, we would have traveled faster, and we could have been there to fight alongside the villagers."

Michael furrowed his eyebrows. "That's crazy. She couldn't have stopped what happened there. She'd undoubtedly be dead. And us too, or maybe recaptured and taken to some dark underworld."

The three men looked over and noticed Rio was awake, staring into the flames without expression, though her hands were tightened as fists.

"Can you tell her that?"

Dr. Saussure calmly spoke to Rio. She listened without speaking at all. Eventually, her clenched fists opened.

\|\|*

The next afternoon, the four travelers paused for a brief rest at an opening in the trees, looking back at the distant lands they had recently traveled. Though they had tried their best to move rapidly, their hike seemed to take forever.

Their path took them steadily and more steeply uphill. Often, they slipped on the loose pine needles, or even had to backtrack to get around impassable cliffs that jutted out suddenly from this arduous land.

It wasn't until now that they had realized how far they had actually come in a long day's march. The last bright rays of the sun reached over the mountain peaks, catching the mottled yellow and orange leaves in a glistening reflection, like that of a disco ball.

Uneasily, Rio pointed downward. Far below, hundreds if not thousands of tiny black dots were mustered in the great open meadow they had walked through just a day earlier. While they watched, a couple of fires sprang up, growing noticeably larger.

"That's an army," Michael said softly. "They're setting up camp for the night." *And they're destroying all those beautiful wildflowers*, he thought. *And where did they suddenly come from? How could we not have noticed a force that large before?*

Bryan was noticeably panicked. He still painfully recalled being a captive, his skin being pinched by the Maugwat and his body bruised by the Bergrisar. He could just imagine hordes of them down there, arguing and fighting among themselves. He had had more than enough of that. "We need to get out of here. Right now."

"An army of that size, it'll take them at least a day to climb up this far," Michael noted. "Maybe two days."

"That's not the point," Travis countered. "They'll send much quicker scouts up after us. We're not armed for a battle against an army or even just a couple of hardened warriors."

Rio spoke rapidly. Bryan, still the quickest at translating, said, "They're tracking us. They've followed the same route we did. Their scouts probably aren't too far behind us even now. We have to get into the higher mountains right away. Our only chance is to keep moving. If we try to find shelter or fortification, we'll never hold out."

The sun was only half an arm's length from dipping below the mountain peaks to the west. They had to push on even with night quickly approaching.

"No fire tonight, no stopping," Rio commanded in her native language. She pointed further ahead and up into the hills. "We must keep going until it is too dark to see any further. If we stop, they'll catch us."

They kept directly behind Rio, their track tightly woven between the thickest trees they could find so it would be unlikely for them to be spotted from far below. Every yard they climbed into the ever-steepening foothills was a battle against gravity, loose soil, and the twilight.

Feet slipped on the bed of pine needles as they forced themselves to push faster. Every tree, every rocky outcropping, was a black shadow.

And then Rio abruptly stopped and held her hands up. The three men behind her nearly—and comically—collided with each other in the near darkness. They each stepped to the side quickly so they could see what had held them up.

There, standing above them on the slope, was a grim native warrior. His hands gripped a thick spear that was easily longer than he was tall. That sharpened spear point was aimed right at them.

The hairy, barrel-chested warrior looked down at the four travelers. The men instantly put their hands up to match their guide and silently looked ahead. There was little more that they could do at that moment. They couldn't run. They couldn't fight.

Rio spoke to the warrior, pointing to herself, her companions, and then off into the distance below in the foothills. Her voice took on a pleading, distressed tone.

Anxiously, the three men watched and waited for a response. None could be sure whether the warrior they had encountered was friend or foe, or if he would be willing to help them or would hold them prisoner until the dark army arrived.

The warrior thought hard for a few moments and looked back past their shoulders. Then, he gave a loud whistle, and with a big bucktoothed grin, he waved them upward.

Chapter 4

Their new guide led them through the thick forest in the nearly complete darkness. The three time travelers could hardly see where they were going, instead choosing to stick as close to Rio as they could. She kept up with the guide, conversing back and forth in their common native tongue so quickly that even Bryan Saussure had difficulty understanding them.

They were stopped several times by more bands of warriors, and soon they were joined by an armed escort of dozens of stocky, hairy men who carried thick spears and were covered in some sort of natural-looking armor.

The first thing they noticed about the village was the burning lights that shined through the tree boughs ahead. The path they were following then left the forest behind. They gazed in wonder at their destination.

Bryan first thought the evening fires danced and glistened as if replicated in mirrors or sheets of polished metal. Then he realized they were simply reflections on water.

The village was set in the center of what appeared to be a wide mountain lake!

The escort of warriors led the four travelers to the water's edge, where they strode upon a long wooden bridge into the village itself.

The three men were astonished at the friendly welcome they were receiving as hundreds of villagers seemed to cram in around them, wanting a better look at the strangers.

Then, through all of the hubbub around them, the three men heard a voice speak in English. Catching their attention in a way that nothing else in this world could, all three of their heads began swiveling, peering through the crowd to find the speaker who knew their language.

***

"Am I really seeing this?" Tommakee said aloud, more to himself in amazement than to anyone else. He hadn't realized he had said it in English.

He quickly rushed through the throng of onlookers. The three boys were quick on his heels, wondering why Tommakee was so interested in these newcomers.

"Travis? Agent Travis? Is that really you?"

"Tom McKey, as I live and breathe," Agent Travis gasped, hardly believing his eyes. The old agency scientist had aged greatly since Travis had last seen him, though he reminded himself that had been over 20 years ago.

The two men shook hands, and then Tom pulled the agent closer in a big bear hug. The three boys smiled, nodding in approval. The rest of the villagers around them also broke into smiles and cheers and pats on the back.

Ono elbowed Kaiyoo. "Reinforcements are here, just like the old tales said they'd come."

"You know this man?" Bryan asked astonished. The odds of encountering someone from the modern world here, 10,000 years in the past, were astronomical.

Travis looked to the two doctors with an incredulous look still on his face. "Do you remember that Professor Charles said that we'd sent men through the portal in the past? One of the men, Agent Mitchell, found his way back through another portal, one occurring in nature. But not everyone who went through was an agent. Let me introduce you to Tom McKey, a scientist and explorer in his own right. He actually chose to go through the agency's portal a long time ago."

Tom smiled. "I've survived through 21 winters in this world. I'm not sure I'd go back now if I was given the choice."

Rio's eyes jumped from one man to the other as the pale-faced men spoke to each other, wide smiles on their happy faces. The one called Tommakee could speak both the common language of the Good People and the language of the pale men fluently.

Introductions were quickly made, and right away the questions began. After realizing the questions weren't going to stop anytime soon, Tom held up his hand to pause their conversation.

"You all look famished," Tom said frowning. Indeed the four newcomers were quite a sight—ragged and torn clothing, dried and cracked skin covered in cuts and abrasions. The men all badly needed shaves. "How long have you been in this world?"

"Just five days," Michael said. "But it feels like weeks."

"We've got to get you fed, and then cleaned up." Tom looked to the three boys and spoke to them in their language. They all nodded and then wiggled their way through the crowd on an urgent mission.

"Those are my boys, sorta my adopted children here. They'll get everything arranged for you. A real welcome party."

"I'm afraid it won't last too long," Travis said soberly. "There's an army gathering, not too far down the foothills. It's huge. I'm afraid we may have led them here. Rio, our guide, can give you all of the details. She's far more in-tune with the lay of the land than we are."

Tom McKey drew in close to the four of them and whispered, "This village is already preparing for possible invaders. We ourselves only arrived recently, and we were chased here by some of the most awful creatures imaginable."

"Nagual," whispered Agent Travis.

"You know of them?" Tom said, looking from face to face.

"It was my assignment to track one back in Michigan, all those years I worked in the field." Agent Travis waved his hand toward his companions. "Michael here encountered a Nagual in a computer virtual reality simulator. Bryan and Rio are well aware of how dangerous the Dogmen can be."

"My point is," Tom whispered, "we don't need to alarm the villagers any more at the moment. It wouldn't be our place to start a panic. Let me escort you to the chief and his war council. They need this information right away. Then they can determine how best to prepare for battle."

***

Despite trying to not to raise an alarm, the newcomers' word of an impending invasion spread through the village like wildfire. It was, after all, a small, tight-knit community.

All preparations were stepped up, all villagers shared a sense of urgency. That next morning, the village was busier than an anthill preparing for winter. Supplies were hauled from the surrounding countryside into the lodges and store huts.

Armed warriors ringed the water's edge, pacing in patrols from the banks up into the forest, where any villagers were collecting the scant resources left even as the harsh cold transitioned the autumn from a time closer to summer to a time closer to winter.

A blanket of light gray clouds obscured the sun, allowing only a cold and lifeless illumination through to the land below.

Onomineese, the young Ahuizotl lookout, told his new friends Kaiyoo and Watotel that many of their warriors were hidden away in the forest, carefully watching all of the game trails that led to their river valley. At the first sign of danger, they would ambush any enemies with their traps first, and then alert the tribe below.

That first alarm was heard just before noon. The deep blare of a horn echoed through the forest to the east. It was joined by other blasts from around the valley.

Immediately, the forest emptied of villagers racing for the bridge into the village. Warriors slowly backpedaled to the water's edge, their weapons at the ready, their faces grim.

Once each of the villagers was safely across, Chief Tialoc gave the sign to cut the village off from the mainland. The main bridge was once again lowered into the depths of the flooded river.

At the edges of the great dam, where it met the mainland on each side of the flooding, dozens of sharpened spear points had been driven into the ground.

The intricate logwork making up the dam was covered in thick, thorny vines, preventing anyone from gaining access to the south end of the village.

The last of the scouts and guards dashed down the main paths to the village. They ran right past the guardians at the shoreline and splashed into the frigid water. Then the warriors joined them, and they all swam for the safety of the outermost ring of the village.

Following predetermined instructions from the chief and his council, all villagers reported in at their family lodges.

Everyone was accounted for.

They were safe now, but isolated.

***

The temperature steadily dropped as the sky grew cloudier and darker. A cold, heavy rain began to fall and the frigid, biting winds whipped down the nearby mountains into the valleys.

Nothing was seen of the enemies for an entire day, even though Ahuizotl guards were posted around the village at all hours of the day and night, carefully scanning the wilderness for signs of movement.

The villagers stayed inside their lodges, still sharpening spears and preserving the last of the land's bounty for what seemed to be a long, besieged winter ahead.

The enemy could be heard, however, moving in the surrounding forest. Occasional shouts and horn blasts gave away their positions, as did the crashing of falling trees. The dark army wasn't ready to show its hand quite yet. They kept to the cover of the thick trees to keep out of sight and out of the elements.

When the storm passed the following afternoon, the dark army finally left the shelter of the forest. They slowly came forth and established themselves in the open space between the water and the trees, laying siege all around the river flooding and the village in its center.

The temperatures hovered right around the freezing point.

As the darkness of the night crept back behind the western mountains, the Ahuizotl village fire pits at the walkways' edges were extinguished. The village disappeared into the blackness of the flooding.

The first night of the siege began.

***

Large bonfires were already blazing in dozens of spots around the edge of the forest in the enemy's camps. Everyone in the Ahuizotl village could hear the enemy's axes chopping over and over as trees fell to fuel the fires that kept them all from freezing.

As the bonfires grew, villagers could see the shadows of the enemy dancing wildly, shouting out war cries.

"What is this devilry?" asked Bryan Saussure.

Tom McKey looked at him somberly. "War party. They're gearing themselves up for battle tomorrow."

"It's a scare tactic, too," Travis added. "Just look around. Look at these people. The warriors might not show much emotion. But the women, the children, the elders...they're all frightened. It doesn't sound like they've ever had an invasion of their village. They've never seen a force like this. They've never seen creatures like these Dogmen."

Michael Camaron shivered. "I'm scared out of my mind. There's a battle coming, and I don't know what is worse—having to endure all of this while we're waiting, or worrying about what will happen once the battle does begin."

Dr. Saussure firmly planted his hand on a railing and stomped one foot upon the decking. "Solid. This whole village is like a castle. No, really, just think about it—it has all of the classic elements of any fortress city from any period in history. Drawbridge that has since been removed. Protective moat around the whole place.

"This place really is impenetrable. And they've prepared themselves to outlast a siege, especially once that biting cold weather hits. That army out there," he pointed across the water, "they'll run out of food well before we do. An army moves on its stomach even more so than it moves on its feet."

Tom McKey shivered. His breath exhaled as a thick cloud. "It's getting colder. Let's get inside. The more we stand here watching them," he pointed at the nearest bonfire, "the more upset we're all going to become."

Bryan agreed. "Good. This cold is nibbling me to the bone, even right through these furs."

Michael Camaron took one last look around at the enemy encampments and the tall spires of flames reaching up toward the endless stars, like glistening diamonds on pitch-black velvet. Then he followed the others into their lodge.

***

Periodically through the starry night, the horrific howl of the Nagual pierced even the loudest of the frenzy occurring all around the flooding. Those howls even rose above the shrieking winds that suddenly reemerged and stoked the flames of the enemy's bonfires into wild, diabolical shapes.

No one slept in the Ahuizotl village.

Far above the earth, the stars twinkled brightly in a completely cloudless sky, allowing the temperature to continue dropping well below freezing.

***

Overnight, the surface of the flooding had frozen. The dark ice was covered by a fine covering of ashes blowing across like a snowstorm from the enemies' bonfires on the western side.

The only open water was the river upstream from the flooding and downstream where it flowed through carefully engineered openings at the base of the dam.

Kaiyoo, Wayotel, and Ono, who had gotten what seemed like only minutes of sleep all night, rose early in the predawn darkness with the rest of the village. By the time they had dressed in the warmest clothing they could find and then slipped outside Ono's lodge, the walkways were already teeming with people.

They would have to settle with watching the battle from one of the inner rings of the village, as only their own Ahuizotl warriors stood guard at the outer ring.

Preparations for battle had moved into their final phase. Villagers flowed in smooth traffic back and forth from the center of the village to the outer edge. They carried supplies of sharpened spears along with loads of rocks, placing them within grasp, just behind their warriors.

More supplies of weapons were stationed at resupply points—which were also potential retreat points—on the walkways and inner rings as well.

All around the village rings, the young ones and the elders, those who could not fight, were sitting on the flat surfaces of the decking, hacking the ends of sturdy branches with stones, sharpening more and more spears of all lengths.

Thick cloud cover arrived with the morning, allowing only weak, gray light to fall upon the world and keeping the land from warming at all.

Everywhere the boys looked, they saw the evil warriors.

The enemy army was already marshaled, standing in loosely gathered formations that completely surrounded the shoreline of the flooding.

Troops of dark men, draped in thick black, shaggy skins and furs, shifted from one booted foot to another. Their faces were covered in either black mud or paint. Their hands gripped their spears and axes and knives, flexing their muscles and lightly jostling each other in anticipation of the battle to come.

Clouds of steamy breath dissipated quickly from both the village and the shore, swept away in the arctic blast of wind that continued whipping down from the mountains.

Everyone except the Dogmen was shivering. These evil creatures seemed to enjoy the weather, their tongues hanging out between sharpened fangs that were pulled back in malevolent smiles as they strode presumptuously among the enemy ranks and contemplated the oncoming battle.

Agent Travis did his best to count heads, and finally, because of the great distance to the shoreline, he settled on a best guess of about a hundred warriors in each troop.

Stalking around these troops, the Nagual growled out orders and communicated with sharp cries back and forth to each other.

Travis leaned over to Tom McKey. "I'd estimate about 2,000 of the human warriors, wouldn't you agree?"

Tom, who had been trying to count them as well, nodded his head slowly. "Yes, at least that number. And it looks like about two dozen Dogmen as well. I'd guess there may be another half as many enemies still hidden in the forest that we can't see."

He was interrupted by a chorus of howls from the Nagual all around the village. On their signal, the dark men began their fierce war cries again, beating against their chests and stomping their thick boots on the hardened ground.

Women and children in the village quickly scattered, heading for the relative safety of their lodges, where at least the war cries were somewhat deadened.

The Dogmen stretched out their long arms toward the village, their claws pointing directly at the Ahuizotl warriors. From behind the main lines of the dark warriors, hundreds of arrows flew high into the gray sky. They arched upward, crisscrossing each other before descending rapidly toward their target.

But the arrows fell short, well short of the village's outer ring. Most impaled in the ice, poking outward like the quills of a porcupine. Some hit the ice and simply bounced in all directions.

The time travelers joined the Ahuizotl people in cheerful shouts.

Not to be outdone, the Nagual motioned for their archers to move right up to the edge of the ice field. A second volley of arrows soon was airborne, but these were still a good couple of paces shy of the wooden walkways.

The Dogmen snarled at each other and then barked out more commands. The archers stepped aside. All around the water's edge, a few of the dark army's scouts cautiously stepped onto the ice.

The villagers waited tensely. The cracking of the ice was loud even against the shrill wind. Most of the scouts made it at least a few feet onto the ice before it broke beneath their weight, plunging them down into waist-high, murky water. A few slid down beneath the surface in the slippery mud of the steep underwater banks, never to be seen again. The rest screeched and scrambled back up the shoreline.

This time, the villagers both shouted and laughed at the enemy's folly.

The Dogmen, however, weren't easily dismayed. They snarled out their next orders, and soon the biggest, most burly of the dark warriors strode up to the water's edge with the smaller archers sitting comfortable upon their shoulders.

At the Nagual's command, they advanced into the water. In only a couple of steps, most were waist high in the freezing water. Some pounded on the ice, breaking it so they could move forward up to their heaving chests. Even from a distance, the Ahuizotl people could see the strain on these powerful warrior's faces as they withstood the water's icy grip.

The archers let loose their next volley of arrows. Their aim wasn't quite as accurate, being perched atop the shoulders of their shivering comrades. But being closer made up for it.

Ahuizotl warriors quickly stepped backward, some tripping over or trampling the gawkers behind them as the arrows slammed downward. The arrows pierced into the walkways, the railings, and even a few found their mark, puncturing the flesh of villagers or guardsmen.

This time it was the Nagual's dark army that sent up the wild cheers and war cries.

But their celebrations were short lived. Even as the archers nocked their second arrows for another round of shots, the huge, powerful men they were mounted upon spasmed in the numbing water. Skin and lips were turning blue. Teeth were chattering. Eyes were rolling back in their heads.

Some slipped on the slimy riverbed while trying to get back to shore. Others were benumbed by the cold, their knees simply buckling beneath them. Still others just passed out, smashing forward into the ice ahead of them.

All around the water's edge, these tandems of warriors and archers fell into the depths of the icy river.

A couple of archers tried desperately to leap to safety but fell ungracefully to their deaths. Only a handful managed to reach the shore, their heavy furs soaked and clinging to their skin, where precious body heat was quickly extracted. They expired of hypothermia shortly afterward.

***

Angrily, the Dogmen glared at the Ahuizotl village with their glowing, yellow, all-knowing eyes. They knew they had been stymied this day. Deep-throated snarls dispatched the dark warriors back to their encampments, where they waited around their burgeoning bonfires.

To a handful of dark warriors the Dogmen gave very specific instructions. These warriors, the fleetest of foot, were immediately sent off into the wilderness on a covert mission.

The Nagual themselves then slipped away into the depths of the forest, to a meeting place all their own, where they secretly contemplated and planned their next assault.

This morning was only a slight delay. They could afford to be patient. The way the weather was currently turning, they could afford to wait until the ice would hold.

Their minds turned to the base needs of sustenance, and they set off to hunt. Their human army was left to its own devices for the time being. The Nagual cared little about the humans, even those they led into battle.

The humans were easily swayed with glory, whether earned by surviving or dying in the fighting. These dark men fought for trinkets, they fought for blood lust. They fought for the promise of something they would never truly gain nor understand.

Humans were easily replaced.

Humans with dark hearts were easily led.

The Dogmen knew the real power in the world. They had fought for millennia, through ages of the world, for their lord Xoloctil who would give them true power over the earth.

The end of this age was coming like the unstoppable advance of winter. More and more of the smaller civilizations were being wiped from the lands. The *Concua Cahuayoh*, the black beast, had finally awoken. It moved through the shadows of the world on its own course, leaving a wide swath of devastation behind it.

With the Nihuatl gone, the world's lesser guardians were no match for the might of the Dogmen and the black beast together.

And soon, their lord Xoloctil would take physical form and completely topple the world, plunging all into chaos with his promise of fire from the sky. Then all would be in darkness.

***

Tom McKey, bundled tightly in furs from head to toe, leaned on the railing outside his lodge and stared across at the bonfires on the northwestern bank of the flooded river.

Raised in the tip of northern Michigan, Tom was very familiar with freezing ice. He had played and skated on frozen rivers, lakes, and ponds all of his childhood.

His father and grandfather had taught him how fast ice would thicken. On cloudless nights with no wind to disturb the water, and given temperatures at or just above 0 degrees, there could easily be an inch of ice formed where there was none the previous day.

Once ice formed, it would grow constantly in the freezing temperatures, especially if there was a good wind to aid it.

That was exactly what was occurring at the moment. The harsh winds had completely died out. The thick cloud cover dissipated just after sunset. Temperatures beneath the bright points of starlight were cold enough to gnaw on exposed flesh.

There was still a little open water in the inner two rings of the village, though skim ice was forming around the edges where the lodges and walkways met the water. The flooding between the outermost ring and the shoreline, however, was already a sheet of ice.

Yesterday we were lucky, Tommakee thought. *With tonight's bitter cold and no wind, the ice may hold the weight of their advance.*

He felt a strong nudge against the small of his back. Smiling in this cold hurt his face, but he couldn't help it. Yuba might be a pain most of the time, but she was still his longtime traveling partner. Though she was lying against the lodge, her long neck could still reach out several feet and make contact.

Tom turned and held her football-shaped head in his fur-covered arms, scratching both beneath her chin and at the top of her head just around her curved horns.

"I'm not sure how we'll get ourselves out of this one, girl," Tom said. "It looks like we're in quite a tight spot."

Yuba gave a low grunt and, in the glare of the nearby kettle light, looked disinterested at pretty much everything in the world at the moment. It could have been 90 degrees out and they might as well have been surrounded by gummy bears for all she cared.

Tom sighed. "Must be nice to be a woolly camel. No responsibilities. No concern for the future. As long as you can get a meal once in awhile, you're good. Even better, you're a survivor, aren't you?"

A moment later, Yuba's long, rough tongue slurped Tom's face. Luckily, most of his skin was covered by a flap of fur akin to a scarf. But his nose and cheeks instantly prickled with pain as the slobber froze into tiny icicles. He wiped his face with the fur of his mittens, saying, "You sure know how to ruin a moment, don't you?"

***

The blackness of night slowly peeled back from the eastern sky, and the old familiar blue of early dawn crept in from between the trees.

Again, the Ahuizotl villagers were awake early, standing close behind their warriors, who stood tall and proud with their weapons at the ready.

Just as the day before, the army of dark warriors marshaled on the shoreline all around the village.

Ono had been given the task of protecting the tribe's honored visitors. It was a task he both revered and secretly detested. It meant he was trusted with the welfare of his new friends, Kaiyoo and Wayotel, as well as their protectors, those pale-faced men, and even the warrior woman.

This strangely assembled band of Good People was called the *Tonauac itolotia*. They had been foretold by the oldest legends as being the saviors of the world. Ono had been chosen by Peshawbe himself as defender of these heroic possessors of the world's light. Ono's duty now lay with them, even over his duty to family and tribe.

And yet Ono wanted to be in the thick of the battle. He wanted to be in the support team for his father and older brother, for the warriors of the village. Ono was sure they would undoubtedly drive this indigent horde back down the hills and scatter them into the wastes beyond.

But that wasn't to be.

The eight of them were all to remain at the lookout atop the center of the great dam, 50 yards away from the southern edge of the village, a quarter mile away from the fighting.

All of them but Yuba, anyway. It was hotly debated whether the sheer weight of Tommakee's beast of burden would break through the ice on the way to the lookout. In the end, Yuba was left sleeping on her wide berth outside the lodge the time travelers had been using.

The humans had carefully made their way in the near darkness to what was undoubtedly the safest location in the flooding.

The lookout was comprised of a wide platform and railing, covering about 40 feet of the dam beneath it. The dam itself was a structural marvel, nearly 20 feet wide at the top and stretching across most of the southern end of the deep river valley.

Huge trees had been strategically placed as an infrastructure with specially carved logs and planks that were engineered to hold back millions of gallons of water.

From the lookout, the heroes could easily look down 30 feet to the frosty soil below. In only a few places did the dam release rivulets of water, the spillways that enabled the river to continue on through the final end of the valley and out of sight behind wooded hills.

And peering back toward the village, they were in position to watch the battle unfold.

***

At the Nagual's command, the first scouts hesitantly stepped out onto the frozen flooding. Their footsteps took them slowly and carefully 5, 10, 20 feet out onto the ice. At a snarl from the nearest Nagual, the scouts tried the thickness of the ice. Several stomped hard with their boots. At least a couple jumped up and down.

Unlike the previous morning, however, the ice held.

The scouts took a tentative look back at their comrades. Then the realization hit them all. It was strong enough to walk on. Maybe not the entire army at one time, but certainly they could send waves of warriors, spaced apart, one wave after another.

The Nagual gave short yipping barks, and the scouts were soon joined by the remaining few dozen archers who had not perished in the previous day's sortie. It didn't take them long to move far enough forward to begin rapidly firing arrows that would easily reach their marks.

At the village, realization hit them quickly as well. Anyone without protection quickly retreated back indoors.

The warriors remaining on guard outside did their best to hide behind makeshift shields, fabricated only hours earlier by the villagers out of cross-hatched branches. These were effective enough to prevent most of the warriors from becoming pincushions.

But plenty of deadly arrows found their way through, causing a good deal of injury and even some deaths.

The three boys, from their vantage point atop the lookout, stared in horror as the lines of enemy archers slowly and steadily moved closer to the village across the ice. All the time, the enemy warriors were able to continue nocking arrows and picking the targets they knew where close enough to hit with accuracy.

Chapter 5

It didn't take long before all of the enemy arrows were spent, but by the time the last bows were lowered, many of these missiles had done plenty of damage.

Slowly, the archers retreated from the ice back to the hard ground. They were replaced by the first line of grisly warriors, who stepped warily onto the ice, weapons in hand.

Their faces were painted with black and gray ash. Crooked, snarling grimaces displayed even more crooked teeth.

More warriors lined themselves along the edge of the ice field, awaiting their turn. The Dogmen would send in one wave at a time to ensure that the ice held.

Slowly the first legion began walking toward the village from both sides of the flooding.

Along the village walkways, severely injured Ahuizotl warriors were pulled back from the front to receive medical treatment.

Wa-Kama and her young apprentices made their way to them as quickly as they could, chanting incantations and handing out a soothing healing paste.

Children were sobbing through doorways as they gazed upon all the blood and the black enemy arrows that had pierced nearly every wooden surface in the outer ring of the village.

Just as the morale of the Ahuizotl seemed about to slip, Chief Tialoc himself strode forward confidently to the easternmost platform and then stepped down onto the ice itself.

He first raised his head to the sky, chanting a prayer to the Great Spirit. Then he extended his long arms wide at his sides. Around him, the warriors rallied.

The chief looked from left to right as his loyal troops spread themselves in a wide curve down on the ice surface, just close enough for their fingers to interlock. A horn blew, and warriors on the western side of the village repeated the maneuver, only centered upon Peshawbe, the chief's most trusted commander.

The Ahuizotl warriors crouched in unison, arms spread out horizontally from their sides. Their heads were bowed, and they began chanting softly to themselves.

Seconds later, their bodies started to quiver, all the way from their exposed toes to their extended fingertips to their bearded faces. Dark hair sprouted all over their skin.

Kaiyoo, Wayotel, and Ono watched in awe as every one of the warriors began to change, to shapeshift into giant beaver guardians!

In the center was their chief, by far the most magnificent of them all. His fur was a sleek reddish-brown marked with thin streaks of gold. Upon his head grew four stubby horns that resembled a crown.

The transformation was complete in moments. Hundreds of these proud Ahuizotl beaver warriors encircled the outermost ring of their village, standing with their thick, furred legs upon the frozen flooding. Behind them, their tails flapped up and down lightly making clicks that reverberated across the ice field.

On the far side of the frozen flooding, a moment of unsurety led the dark army to pause, watching the Ahuizotl transformation. A couple of the biggest brutes gave a twisted sneer, some of them spitting in the direction of their opponents.

Emboldened by the stability of the ice, the dark warriors marched forward. Then, at a growling command from the Dogmen behind them, the first wave of evil men shouted their piercing war cries and began to race forward, spears raised to attack.

***

The beaver guardians, evenly spaced along the ice, turned their backs to the onrushing enemy. They crouched, their thick legs widened for maximum stability.

"What are they doing?" Kaiyoo nearly yelled, turning to Onomineese in a panic. He couldn't believe the tribe's best warriors were turning their backs to the enemy.

But his new friend just smiled and pointed. "Watch."

The beaver guardians stood their ground, holding the line and patiently waiting. The boys could see the muscles beneath their furred legs rippling, their clawed feet digging into the ice for purchase. Their wide, flat tails quivered just above the ice.

The war cries of the advancing army rose in unison as they broke into an all-out charge. The second line of warriors waited no longer and began rushing across the ice as well, as it was holding their weight just fine.

And at that point, less than a stone's throw away, the guardians acted.

As one, they snapped their huge tails up into the air and sent them crashing down upon the ice. The crack of the impact echoed through the valley. But after that initial blast, Kaiyoo understood their strategy.

The ice field splintered out away from the guardians, spider-webbing toward the onrushing enemy soldiers. The cracking became nearly deafening as the shockwave blasted its way through the ice.

Trapped by their own blood lust, the first line of enemy soldiers tried to pull up and even attempt a retreat, but they were slammed forward by the warriors behind them. And then they all began to disappear, slipping and sliding into the frigid water beneath the chunks of ice that were now bobbing like acorns in a stream.

***

A chorus of cheers went up from the villagers, and it was repeated over at the lookout by Ono, Kaiyoo, and Wayotel.

Agent Travis only smiled, thinking how perfectly these Ahuizotl people lived in balance with their environment and the abilities they possessed. They could defend their homes no matter what might be thrown at them.

Most of the beaver guardians disappeared into the icy waters too, but their newly transformed bodies were made to withstand the conditions. They joyfully swam in and around the ice chunks playfully pushing them around and smashing them toward the shore. Any last remaining enemies who were clinging to chunks of ice were knocked off balance into the deep, freezing water.

Not a single dark warrior made it back to shore. Any enemies who tried swimming back, despite succumbing to the inevitable hypothermia, were attacked from beneath the surface by the giant beavers and pulled down to their doom.

With the first two waves of human enemies defeated, and the village secured from attack once again, the giant beavers swam back to the wooden walkways of the outer circle. They were greeted by cheers from the villagers, who had come forth to celebrate. Some of the beaver guardians stayed in the water, though most shimmied their way back up onto the walkways.

***

Back at the lookout, the heroes were jubilant, too. But it was short lived.

A sound like the rumble of thunder began to slowly crescendo around them.

"What is that noise?" Bryan Saussure said aloud, looking both directions across the flooding at the remaining dark army still stationed on either bank.

The others started scanning the land and forests beyond the flooding, trying to locate what was causing that sound to build. They could even feel it, a vibration in the very logs of the dam, in the very earth around them.

Onomineese turned and gazed south at the valley floor some distance below. "Oh no," he gasped.

"What is it?" asked Tommakee who, anticipating trouble, had instinctively pulled up his thick walking staff. He stepped over to the railing where Ono was standing and was quickly joined by the others.

But Ono was beyond words. He simply pointed one arm out ahead. Next to him, Rio stared out at the river valley, her mouth opened in shock.

Three mythic beasts, huge and powerful, were galloping up the valley floor along the muddy banks of the creek below.

Not one of the boys had ever seen such creatures. Each creature was twice the height of a man and covered in a long, thick, blackish-gray fur that rippled backward from the breeze generated by their forward charge. A single horn, easily as long as Wayotel was tall, pointed forward from each beast's head.

Of course the men from the future knew immediately these were the famed woolly rhinoceros, and this fully cemented their theory that they were indeed at least 10,000 or more years in the past.

Riding each beast was a dark warrior, equally decked out in long, black fur. Even from a distance the boys could see the wild plumage of feathers and beads streaking back from the men's heads and necks.

These riders sat upon makeshift saddles that allowed them to lean forward, knifing into the wind. There were no bridles, Dr. Saussure noted. The riders simply grasped long handfuls of the beasts' fur.

Only 500 yards and less than a minute away from impact, the riders shouted to their steeds and the beasts lowered their massive heads and horns, reaching maximum velocity.

***

"Are those woolly rhinos?" Michael Camaron started to ask, but he was interrupted by the astonished voice of Dr. Saussure.

"*Elasmotherium*, as I live and breathe," the doctor exhaled. He turned, smiling, to his younger colleague. "Woolly rhinoceroses were only native to Europe and Asia. This is a related sub-species. True, it's a forerunner of the modern rhinoceros, but not quite the one you're thinking about. I must admit I've never read of any discoveries that demonstrated so much hair. It has really been quite an argument among paleobiologists, you know, and even then only circumstantial evidence has ever been put forward. It must be an adaption to the climate, after all..."

"We don't have time for a history lecture," Agent Travis said forcefully, pointing at dark fur pelts that were tied around the rhino's heads. "Their eyes are covered. They don't intend to slow down. When they hit the dam, this whole village is going to be swept away in the surge."

The doctor turned his head and furrowed his eyebrows. "But why would they collide into the dam? That wouldn't make much sense."

Onomineese understood immediately, even though he couldn't translate Travis's words. The boy's head darted quickly in a couple of directions toward the nearest village huts. "There!" Onomineese yelled, grabbing Kaiyoo's arm and pulling him toward the nearest walkway of the village.

The others didn't hesitate to follow, though Travis had to yank on the awestruck doctor's arm to pull him away. Ahead of them was a stack of long birch bark canoes, tied upside-down to a dock for winter storage.

Seconds seemed an eternity as the eight of them raced across the ice field as fast as their slipping feet could take them.

Though the ice at the south end of the flooding was still intact, its integrity had been compromised by the Ahuizotl warriors. Michael's eyes widened in fear as the ice creaked and groaned beneath their weight. Cracks spider-webbed outward from their foot falls toward the bobbing ice chunks in the distance.

Yet then they were all at the nearest landing. Rio and the boys made it first, easily leaping up onto the wooden structure. Tommakee and Michael Camaron were only steps behind.

Agent Travis dove, pulling Bryan Saussure with him through the air, just as the ice was giving way beneath his feet. They both slid across the wooden planks that were covered in frost.

It took only a moment for Rio to slice the ropes. Two long canoes were quickly overturned and pointed toward the dam. Rio and all three boys grabbed wide-bladed paddles from the decking before everyone piled in. Just as Tommakee and Travis slipped into the back ends, each snagging their own paddle along the way, they all heard the deafening crash below.

***

The horned beasts, spurred on by their masters, simultaneously drove their long, spiked horns right into the superstructure of the log dam. With their eyes covered, they never knew what they had hit.

The momentum of each rhinoceros drove its thick skull right into the intricately stacked logs despite the sudden release of enormous pressure from within.

So intent on their mission, the riders held on the entire way. These evil men were impaled on the sharpened logs as the bodies of the beasts completely disappeared within the lower structure of the dam, so dynamic was the thrust of their impact.

And with an explosion of the greatest magnitude, the dam gave way.

The potential energy stored up in the water burst out into all directions. At the base of the dam, the three sacrificial beasts and their riders were ripped to shreds, buried beneath the weight of wood, stone, and mud. The upright wall buckled, split by three great cracks from the impacts at the base.

But the fissures didn't end with the dam. A second later, the thicker ice surrounding the village exploded in a shower of water spray, wood splinters, and tiny daggers of ice.

The three great cracks became one massive hole as the force of the water blew everything outward. Millions of gallons of water exploded, burying everything in the deep valley. The lookout and much of the upper walkway completely disappeared beneath the spray.

Chief Tialoc and the warriors swung their heavy, furred bodies around, staring at the eruption behind them. Logs thick as a man's leg were firing up into the air amid the cloud of destruction that mushroomed up at the dam.

Water and ice chunks gushed out the eastern end of the village, where the thickness of the dam wall could no longer be seen.

Even a quarter mile away at the battlefront, it only took a second for the force of the blast to rupture any remaining ice beneath and around the village foundations. Now the Ahuizotl people faced the same trouble they had dealt to their enemies only minutes ago.

Already the huts and their log foundations, the work of decades that had kept the village impenetrable to invasion, were being swept away in moments in the roiling water.

Plunged into the icy water, the beaver guardians were not as susceptible as the humans to harm. But the once placid flooding had become a churning cauldron of jagged ice and logs, as well as every bit of floating debris. Even sharp tools, utensils, and other implements swirled through the now rushing stream, slicing and spearing the villagers.

Those villagers who couldn't transform, however, were in dire peril. Most of the women and children were already cowering within the lodges. They were swept away, drowning beneath the thick stew of materials that once created their homes.

The warriors instantly forgot their enemy at the doorstep and instead plunged into the murky depths, over and over, searching frantically for their families.

And still, the water flowed out through the gaping hole where the ancient dam once stood.

***

The last thing Onomineese saw as he looked back past the center of the village were the arms of the evil army on the river bank raised with their triumphant war cries as they rushed toward the draining home of the Ahuizotl people. Already the water level of the flooding was dropping significantly.

Tommakee gave one last look back, his eyes searching for Yuba. The shaggy camel was nowhere in sight. *I guess this is where we part ways, old friend*, Tommakee thought depressingly.

Then the canoe riders rocked backward violently as the two craft lurched forward in the rush of water.

Tommakee and Travis paddled and steered from the back, more to maneuver them around the flotsam than for propulsion. They were aided by Rio and Ono paddling at the front of one canoe, while Kaiyoo and Wayotel stroked from the front of the other.

Neither of the two scientists had paddles to use. Dr. Saussure was, as usual, terrified by all of the excitement. He cringed low in the canoe behind Wayotel.

Michael Camaron, on the other hand, was an avid outdoorsman with many adventures in canoeing over the years. But without a paddle, he could only grip the gunwales tightly, trying to balance out his girth. The only thought he had was wondering how many millions of gallons of water were there behind the dam.

There was no other direction to head but on through the gap in the dam wall. They couldn't paddle fast enough to escape the gushing water. There had not really been much time for a plan anyway—the canoes had only offered a last-ditch escape.

Travis had just a moment to look over at Tommakee in the other canoe. They both nodded to each other, then began to stroke with all their might.

***

The rush of escaping water had created a waterfall of about 20 feet to the ever-widening river below. Already the little creek had swollen to a turbulent river, raging down the valley.

"Lean back!" Michael shouted, realizing the only way to avoid capsizing was to keep the canoes as horizontal as possible. He reached out and grabbed Ono's shoulders, pulling the boy backward. Luckily in the other canoe, both Wayotel and Dr. Saussure did their best to flatten themselves and hold on tightly to the gunwales.

Unlike the nearly straight vertical drop of a true waterfall, this powerful cascade of water burst outward, easing the canoes' descents. But all of the occupants felt their stomachs lurch as gravity took over through their forward momentum.

Then, the canoes both fell amid the dirty water and debris on all sides. Despite their best efforts and the natural physics of the breached dam, the canoe prows both managed to tip forward and plunge beneath the water below.

Rio and Kaiyoo were both completely submerged, but they managed to keep a grip on their paddles while digging their knees into the sides of the canoe to keep from being ejected. And then they bobbed back up, each sputtering as they tried to catch their breath, which had been exhaled with the freezing cold water.

Wayotel, soaked head to toe, miserably spat out water as his fingers kept a death-grip on the sides of the canoe.

Water sprayed outward in all directions. The paddlers, soaked and shivering, shook the drops out of their eyes but pushed onward with all their might. The two canoes, laden with frigid water, still stayed afloat though they were very difficult to maneuver in the rushing current.

"Bail!" Michael shouted over at Dr. Saussure only a few feet away. The scientist had taken quite a wave directly in the face and he was still sputtering. Yet a moment later, he was scooping the water out of their canoe as quickly as his cupped hands could muster.

Tommakee and Travis shouted at each other over the din around them, trying their best to navigate a passage downstream. The newly widened river was more than spacious enough for both canoes to travel adjacently.

The problem, of course, was the debris all around. The rushing current had worn away the riverbank, uprooting whole trees while carrying away anything that slipped into the water. The flotsam slammed into the canoes, jostling the passengers and threatening to capsize the already overloaded craft.

Luckily the current was strong, such as this valley hadn't seen in decades, perhaps centuries, since the Ahuizotl people had built their village stronghold. Tommakee was just starting to feel a bit of relief when something zipped before his face. His head snapped back in surprise. He blinked several times, and then he realized what it was.

An arrow.

Thwak! This time, Agent Travis looked down and saw the shaft of a thick, black arrow protruding through the skin of his canoe. The sharpened stone point stopped only inches from his left thigh.

Soon arrows were zipping all around them, raining down from the woods high up on the river's left bank. Instinctively, the two men who were steering directed their craft to the river's far right bank, and most of the arrows fell into the water. But they could see it wouldn't take much more for the archers, hidden among the thick cedars, to adjust their aim.

"Row! Row!" the men in the back yelled. Those with paddles threw all of their strength behind every stroke, leaning forward with their momentum. Tommakee's canoe shot ahead, and in only seconds they sped in tandem. This exposed both canoes yet allowed them both to stay as far from the left bank as possible.

"Bail! Bail!" Michael Camaron answered. He slapped and splashed the water from his canoe, just as Bryan Saussure cupped water with his now shaking hands, doing his best to toss it out.

No matter how fast everyone paddled, the canoes couldn't increase speed while weighted down with gallons of water.

There was no way the canoes could beach safely on the right bank, yet there was no safety in the water.

Arrows continued to hit the river's surface only inches from each of the craft. Occasionally one found its mark and pierced one of the canoe's hulls.

Kaiyoo, in the front of Tommakec's canoe, felt his arms aching. He knew he had to keep going, but he didn't know how much longer he could keep paddling. He wished for more strength, for more to fall back upon. He wished for the strength of the bear guardian deep within his soul, he wished to be able to change.

Oh, how he would swim fearlessly across this river, thunder up the bank, and maul all of the enemies. They would never hide from him—he would sniff them all out and make them pay for the damage they had done to this world.

The change didn't happen, probably for the best. If Kaiyoo had transformed at that moment, the canoe would have certainly been demolished beneath his weight and bulk and everyone likely would have drowned.

But luckily, he found a little more inner strength to push forward. At that moment, feeling a bit reinvigorated, Kaiyoo looked ahead. And then his heart sank.

The steep banks narrowed in close to the river forming a rocky cliff towering up 50 feet on either side. Perched all along the left cliff were archers, like gulls among the crags.

Finally lighter from the constant bailing, the two canoes rushed forward, closing the distance. The two canoes pulled up alongside each other.

Kaiyoo remembered his father's tales of hunting the huge malmuks as winter approached their village. One group of hunters spooked the great, tusked beasts, driving them forward as fast as their thick legs could carry them.

All along the predestined route, more and more hunters created a frenzy until the malmuks rushed right into the trap awaiting them. With no place else to go, the beasts smashed into each other as they tumbled down a rocky precipice. Bones splintered while the huge bodies piled up.

Once they were immobile, the hunters made short work of them.

Now, Kaiyoo and his companions were the prey headed straight for the hunters' trap. There was no stopping it from happening—the river's surge was even stronger now. Every second was another canoe length closer to the inevitable.

In just moments, the others too saw their doom looming ahead. There was nothing they could do.

On the rocky bank, the archers, decked in all black like the evil warriors who were currently raiding the Ahuizotl village far back in the distance, raised their bows and nocked their arrows.

Wayotel dropped his paddle into the canoe amid the water that already sloshed around his ankles. He raised his arms up wide over his head and closed his eyes, already beginning to chant softly.

The archers pulled back their strings.

Dr. Saussure squinted his eyes tightly and covered his face with his arms.

Rio thought of her dead husband and brother, wondering how long it would take before she would be joining them in the great land beyond.

Michael Camaron scowled, wondering how he had ever ended up in such a predicament. Becoming a pincushion in some far-off realm of time and space that may or may not have really existed wasn't exactly the way he thought his life had been heading.

Agent Travis calmly thought this was a fitting end for his most unusual life of adventure, for all of the pure craziness he had ever been through in chasing the world's mythic creatures.

Bowstrings snapped. Arrows shot out into the air above the river.

***

There may have been only two dozen archers releasing two dozen arrows, but to the passengers in the canoe, the impending projectiles seemed to blacken out the gray sky above. They all followed Dr. Saussure's lead in instinctively raising their hands, crossing arms at the wrists, in a vain attempt at protection.

All of them except Wayotel, that is. The boy's arms were spread wide, hands and fingers splayed outward, like a huge target. Nearly half of the archers had even taken specific aim at the boy whose outstretched arms provided a perfect focal point.

The arrows bolted right at their targets, seemingly right on the mark.

And then, they all stopped in mid-air, embedded in the supernatural force of Wayotel's shield spell.

The archers glanced angrily at each other, and then quickly nocked more arrows, firing at will. These had no effect either. Wayotel's spell fully covered both canoes.

Tommakee was the first to peer out between his fingers. He was filled with stark amazement, first at still being alive and second at the sight of dozens of arrows paused midflight only a few feet above them.

His amazement was short lived, however. There was no time to wait and see how long the boy could keep the spell going. "Row! Row! Row!" Tommakee yelled to the others.

***

The canoes, still protected by Wayotel's invisible spell, passed the lines of archers, who continued madly pouring dozens of their arrows at their seemingly unassailable targets.

Then suddenly the archers stopped. They lowered their bows and stared at the runaway canoes, even though they were still well within range. Not a single enemy warrior made effort to chase the escapees. Not a one even moved from where he was standing.

A fierce roar filled the entire river valley. It drowned out the rough splashing of oars and water around them.

Above the canoeists, flocks of large, black birds took to the air from the tall pines lining the steep cliffs on each side of the river.

Kaiyoo's heart dropped and all air escaped from his chest. He knew that sound. He had heard it in his nightmare.

Everyone shuddered. Looking down at them from one rocky, barren precipice about 50 yards ahead, where the river bent to the right, was the black beast.

"Waheela," Rio softly breathed, just audible enough for Michael Camaron to hear.

Its black, pebbly skin was so dark that it appeared oily, almost shimmering.

Indeed, to Agent Travis's mind, the creature conjured up images of a black hole, as if it was absorbing all of the daylight around itself, into itself.

"You've got to be kidding me!" Michael sputtered after being splashed by a faceful of water. "There's something even worse than those Dogmen?"

***

Only Wayotel seemed oblivious to the Waheela, as he concentrated on his protection spell with all his might.

The Waheela showed its rows of needle-like teeth as it roared again. Its body then twisted side to side as it unfurled a pair of wide, bat-like wings from along its back.

It's molting, Dr. Saussure thought. *Like an incomplete metamorphosis in insects. The wings are newly expanded from its skin.*

And like an insect tentatively trying out its new wings, the Waheela gave them a stretch and a shake.

It gave a jump into the air, and despite beating its wings tremendously, they weren't quite ready to support its weight.

With flight beyond its current capability, the Waheela raised its wings high, snarled, and leapt from the cliff toward the canoes in the river below.

Its wings may not have supported the creature for flying, but they were still highly effective for gliding. Faster than a predatory bird, the Waheela dove toward its prey.

***

Kaiyoo stood up, his back against Wayotel's. His arms extended wide in an exact match to his Tonal. He closed his eyes and felt the power, their combined power, rush outward.

Behind them, Bryan Saussure crouched perfectly still so as to balance the canoe and keep it steady. He pinched his eyes shut tightly.

The shield spell intensified, covering the canoes in a bright white light extending around them all like a sphere.

Red eyes blinded, the black beast peeled its head up and away from the protective sphere. And then the impact came.

The Waheela couldn't penetrate the shield, but its rocketing body was still forceful. It slammed the canoes downward into the deep water. The humans frantically grabbed the gunwales to keep themselves from being cast out.

Wayotel and Kaiyoo, standing together and concentrating on their spell, were thrown up into the air, precariously toward the madly rushing water. Tommakee stared in horror, powerless to help the two boys.

And then, out of nowhere it seemed, Dr. Saussure stopped cringing in the middle of the canoe. He dove forward grasping both boys and falling with them to the relative safety of the bow of the craft.

Agent Travis just happened to have looked in that direction, and deep in his heart he was impressed. It was the most courageous, selfless thing he had seen the doctor do since he had met him.

Having been deflected uncontrollably away, the Waheela arrowed headfirst into the gravelly soil where the river met the bank. Its own impact was tremendous enough to cause a landslide that buried most of its body seconds later.

The canoes, though mostly filled with water again, continued downstream away from the beast. For a second time, the escapees frantically bailed water until they were exhausted. The canoes continued speeding along the river, quickly outpacing their enemies.

Epilogue

Epilogue

The morning passed by as the two canoes continued their sprint down the river. Aided by the rushing water, they put considerable distance between themselves and the now-ruined Ahuizotl village.

Rio refused to give up her paddle or her position in the front of her canoe. They had stopped briefly twice already to switch positions and thus individually rest their aching muscles. But each time one of the men offered to take her place, she just silently shook her head.

Her thoughts kept returning to the trail of destruction extending backward into her past. The ruined Ahuizotl village behind them. Before that, the ruined village of her friends, the Nesatin, whose restless spirits were already rising from the dead.

The death of the little girl who she knew by face but not by name. And before that, the deaths of her brother and her husband, to whom she had just been married the night of the Sun Festival.

She thought back to the deaths of so many before that fateful day when the Great Spirit delivered the pale-faced men just as she had seen in her many premonitions. Death and destruction lined the path back to her earliest childhood, further back than she could even remember.

Her mind was still a mix of internally roiling emotions. She had been trained from the youngest age to bury her feelings, to hide the emotions, to concentrate on the present moment. The role was always to serve, to protect. She accepted this without question.

The Great Spirit had chosen her specifically for some bigger purpose in the world, of that she was now certain. Why else would she have dreamed for years of the coming of the pale-faced men? How else could she have known there would be four of them altogether, even though only three appeared from the depths of the glowing water at the place of the standing stones?

She turned her head ever so slightly to look at the two youngest boys in the other canoe. Could this Kaiyoo really be the boy of whom the legends spoke? Could he really be the great golden bear she had seen in her dreams, the one who would lead the pale-faced men to challenge the armies of darkness?

***

Agent Travis was now taking his turn to rest in the middle of the canoe. He laid back, exhausted after two full turns steering and paddling. At his age, this was by far the toughest workout he had had in years.

His mind kept returning to the army of Dogmen. His experience had only been tracking a single Nagual. To have seen a dozen or more prowling the ranks of the dark army was as horrific as it was impressive. These weren't just solitary, mindless killing machines.

The Nagual were the leaders of legions. They were powerful, and driven, and relentless.

And from his own experiences, having studied and tracked a Dogman over the course of his career, Travis knew there was little, if anything, that could stop them.

In all likelihood, the Dogmen were already on their trail again.

Not just the Dogmen, he thought. *That Waheela creature too. As soon as it's able to fly, we're all in deep trouble.*

He sighed and closed his eyes. *Dogmen. Waheela. Guardians of all types. What other mythological beasts are still out there in the wilderness that we haven't encountered yet?*

***

After several hours of paddling, the rushing water began to calm down and the river widened. As they rounded a curve, Rio and Bryan Saussure, at the front of their canoes, were the first to see the long lake extend before them. It was ringed with thick forest, and now that the land had opened up, they could all see the peaks of a mountain chain not too far in the distance.

Michael Camaron, paddling directly behind Bryan, tapped his fellow scientist on the shoulder. "Do you see the gap in the mountains?" He pointed up over the treeline.

Bryan nodded. "I'm assuming that's the pass we'll head for first."

The paddling was even more difficult now because the current had disappeared far below the surface. With throbbing muscles, the paddlers gave their last efforts to reach the northeastern shoreline.

***

The heroes climbed out of their canoes a few feet from shore. The water was translucent but the bottom was sandy and fairly firm. They pulled the canoes up onto the bank and into the cover of the thick trees, hiding them beneath the underbrush.

Once the canoes were safely stashed out of sight, Rio and the three boys brushed and smoothed the sand and soil to hide the tracks of their feet and the dragged canoes. No one would be able to tell that they had come ashore.

Tommakee led the older men to quickly gather downed wood and to start a smokeless fire. The boys had been shivering steadily over the last stretch of river. When they landed, Wayotel's lips were turning blue. Tommakee knew they needed a fire's warmth to dry their clothing and prevent hypothermia.

It didn't take long before a wide, low fire was glowing beneath the tree canopy far from any potential peering eyes that might have followed them down the long stretch of river. The thick curtain of surrounding evergreens helped keep the fire's warmth close to their bodies.

The entire company had stripped down to just their minimal undergarments, and all of the rest of their clothing was stretched over bent saplings to dry. Wayotel was huddled between the other two boys and soon his shivering stopped.

Rio silently sat near the fire, slowly drawing a chunk of rock along one paddle blade. Every few strokes, she carefully sliced its now fine edge through the red embers and then through the soft black dirt. In but a short time, she had turned two of those useful tools into keenly edged weapons.

Though she was now a companion to these travelers, she still felt apart from them. Not connected to them, at least not quite yet. She sat apart from them for the time being, lost in her own thoughts.

The four pale-skinned men were all sitting close to each other and as near to the fire as they could get.

"Where do we go from here?" asked Bryan.

"We need help," Michael said looking to Tommakee and Agent Travis. "We need reinforcements. We can't do this on our own. We can't fight against an army like that back there."

Agent Travis sighed. "We can run, but not for too long. We did get a nice head start, but they'll be back after us again."

"Those Dogmen, that Waheela creature. They'll all be after us," Bryan said and shivered. "They tracked us before. They'll find us again."

Tommakee thought deeply for a minute, remembering their evening in Chief Tialoc's council lodge. "The story from Wa-Kama. We need to reach the Ocelotl. We need the help of the jaguar warriors. The Ocelotl guardians are the only thing left in the world that can defeat the Nagual." Remembering the four natives seated around them, Tommakee translated into their common language.

"But they're so far away," Kaiyoo said, feeling defeated. "The Nagual are everywhere. How will we ever get to the Ocelotl now?"

Tommakee slowly looked around at everyone. Only Rio seemed withdrawn from the conversation as she concentrated on her work of making weapons.

The old wayfarer said, "The only way, the safest way, is to cross the mountains. The Dogmen fear the mountains. If we can get to the other side, perhaps we'll be safe enough to escape south. If we stay on this side, they will catch us for sure."

Once his words were translated, everyone around the fire nodded. It was as good a plan as any they could think of.

Just as Rio was raising her head to share her agreement, a noise in the distance startled them all.

The boys instinctively flattened themselves along the ground. The noise continued, getting closer. They heard twigs snapping and smaller saplings whipping back after they were bent by whatever was approaching.

"Something big's coming," whispered Ono.

Rio crouched with her sharpened canoe paddle pointed forward. The other four men grabbed paddles from the pile. Tommakee stepped in front of the boys at the ready. There was nowhere they could outrun an enemy now. They would have to make a stand and fight to the finish right here.

***

A deep grunt emanated from the woods before a shaggy, round head poked through the thick underbrush of the evergreens.

"Yuba!" Tommakee nearly yelled. "How did you get here?" He and the three boys all jumped forward to hug the camel as she pushed through the boughs toward the fire.

Yuba's fur dripped water all over them, though luckily she didn't shake it off and douse them all. Tommakee led her over to the fire where the horned camel plopped down and promptly began to doze off.

The humans would never know what adventures she had been through, but they could tell it had been enough to wear her out.

Despite her wet fur, the three boys all laid against her warm bulk, rising and falling with each deep breath she took. Tommakee sat by Yuba's head, scratching her ears and the spots where her horns grew out of her head. He was speechless at the moment.

Rio gave a half smile before handing one of the sharply bladed paddles to Agent Travis along with her stone. She pointed to the rest of the paddles now lying nearby, and they nodded at each other.

Before turning and slipping away into the forest, she said in the common native tongue, "Finish these. I'm going to get some food." Of course, Tommakee and the boys knew what she had said. But the three newer time travelers were amazed at how much they had all begun to understand the native language, now that they had been so immersed in it.

***

The company kept hiking, as quickly as their feet could take them. Even in the cold, late afternoon air, the time travelers were already sweating profusely as the land began to rise steadily again.

Their break had been perfectly long enough to rest, dry their clothing, and share a few bites of skewered squirrel that Rio brought back and cooked for them. They were as ready as they would ever be to truly begin their journey together.

Now, Rio led them on, following what appeared to be a game trail up into the higher elevations. Tommakee and Yuba were right behind her.

The boys walked next, and were followed up by Travis, Bryan, and Michael, who dragged pine branches behind them in the hopes of hiding the footsteps of Yuba and the rest of the party.

As afternoon wore on toward early evening, tiny snowflakes began to fall from the gray sky. Tommakee, his arms outstretched and his hands opened upward, spoke first in the native language, and then translated for his modern-day companions. "Looks like autumn has finally passed us by. We've been short-changed. Winter's here already."

Rio held up her hand to stop the company. Slowly, she walked a few paces forward before pausing and crouching down to examine something on the ground ahead. Light snow fell upon her black hair.

"Stiyaha," the warrior woman said softly, pointing at the ground in front of her. She gave them all an incredulous look. "Stiyaha."

Tommakee tilted his head and shrugged his shoulders. After a few moments of silence, Yuba gave a grunt and then started forward, towing her master onward up the game trail. It was decided—they would move ahead.

The three young boys ran up once Rio moved back into the lead position. Travis walked up to the spot Rio had examined and exhaled deeply at the sight. He then quickly caught up to Tommakee, and the two began a deep conversation.

A few steps later, Michael Camaron and Bryan Saussure caught up to the boys, who were still gawking at the spot on the ground. Michael leaned over to Bryan and asked, "What did she say?"

But Dr. Saussure didn't answer him. Instead, he put one flat hand on Michael's chest to stop him. Then he pointed at his feet. The boys had finally moved out of the way so they could see it for themselves.

The soft soil from the recent rains had captured one singular, solitary footprint. It was a few days old, but there was no mistaking it.

It had a human shape to it, five toes clearly outlined in the now dried mud. But the track from toe to heel was as long as Michael's forearm, from elbow to fingertip.

"Stiyaha?" Michael mouthed the word, trying his best to mimic the pronunciation.

As the tiny snowflakes became steadily larger and more numerous, the doctor translated. "We're in Bigfoot country."

About the author:

With an English degree from Michigan State University and a master's degree in educational leadership from Central Michigan University, Frank Holes, Jr. spends his days as an elementary principal in northern Michigan. He lives with his wife Michele, son James, and daughter Sarah.

All five of Frank's previous Dogman novels have been enjoyed by readers in and around the Great Lakes region and across the country. And both novels in his children's fantasy series, The Longquist Adventures, have been a hit with elementary students through adults.

See all of Frank's novels on his website:

http://www.mythmichigan.com

About the cover artist & illustrator

Craig Tollenaar lives in southwest Michigan with his wife Traci and his daughters Isobel and Stella, and a peculiarly skinny dog named Ruby. He earned a Bachelor of Arts from Alma College and has been working as a creative artist of some sort for some time.

He spends much of his day with any type of instrument that makes a mark on a page. He enjoys living in the Midwest (and its meteorological uncertainties) and an occasional good time. Craig's impressive artwork can also be seen on the covers of *Year of the Dogman*, *The Haunting of Sigma*, *Nagual: Dawn of the Dogmen*, as well as the cover and interior pictures from *Tales From Dogman Country*, *The Dogman Epoch: Shadow and Flame*, and in both novels *Western Odyssey* and *Viking Treasure* in the series The Longquist Adventures.

About the editor

Daniel A. Van Beek believes that we must harness the power of punctuation and never hesitate to grapple with grammar. He is the author of one book and has served as editor on many others, both fiction and nonfiction. A graduate of the University of Michigan, Daniel is obsessed with not only Wolverine sports teams but also the peculiarities of vintage base ball and long beards. While a craftsman with words, he enjoys the work of creators in every medium, whether it be paint, wood, music, food, or beer. Daniel lives with his wife Jennifer, his son Ezra, and his daughters Lois and Sylvia, in Benton Harbor, Michigan.

Made in the USA
Middletown, DE
10 October 2016